Shoreline of Infinity

Issue 2 Winter 2015/16

Science fiction magazine from Scotland

ISSN 2059-2590

Subscriptions to Shoreline of Infinity are available. Visit the website for details.

Shoreline of Infinity is available in digital or print editions. Submissions of fiction, art, reviews, non-fiction are welcomed: contact the editor via the website.

Publisher
The New Curiosity Shop
Edinburgh
Scotland
v081215

Contents

Cover: Sara Ljeskovac

Editorial Team

Editor-in-Chief:
Noel Chidwick
Art Director:
Mark Toner
Deputy Editor/Poetry Editor:
Russell Jones
Reviews Editor (from Issue 3):
Iain Maloney
First Reader:
Monica Burns
Assistant Editor(web and social media):
Anna Williamson

First Contact
Web:
www.shorelineofinfinity.com
Email:
contact@shorelineofInfinity.com
Twitter: @shoreinf
and on Facebook

Pull up a Log

Thanks to all of you who read and enjoyed the very first issue of *Shoreline of Infinity*. We were delighted by your positive comments, humbled by your enthusiasm and fired up by your encouragement. Issue 1 was a test to see if we could produce a science fiction magazine and find a readership. We did, and could and hence you hold Issue 2 in your hands. From now on *Shoreline of Infinity* will be published quarterly at the equinoxes and the solstices - subscribe, and never miss an issue.

When Art Director Mark Toner and I started the magazine we hoped to attract talent to support us; immediately Edinburgh poet and writer Russell Jones offered his help, and over a cup of coffee and a muffin we offered him the role of poetry editor. Russell accepted, and hence we have a new science fiction poetry section, we begin with poems from two of Scotland's science fiction writers, Ken MacLeod and Iain Banks. But Russell showed other talents and organised a great launch party for the magazine featuring poetry, story readings, art and SF songs from Painted Ocean.* Folk enjoyed the night so much we were asked when we were going to put on the next one: as a result we are now running science fiction evenings in Edinburgh on the last Thursday of the month at Deadhead Comics. If you are in Edinburgh, do come along.

Our SF Caledonia feature this issue focuses on Duncan Lunan as he reaches his 70th birthday. Duncan is best know for his books on astronomy and space, but he has had a strong influence on science fiction writers in Scotland. Paul F Cockburn talks to Duncan about his writing life, and we include a previously unpublished story, *Last Days in the Nanotech Wars*.

But *Shoreline of Infinity* stretches beyond Edinburgh and Scotland. As in Issue 1, this issue features stories some fine new writers from Australia, Canada, England, Norway, Scotland and USA. Likewise we have artists from Scotland, Switzerland and USA. This is important to us, and especially now with so much speechifying of bombings, war and terrorists drenching the media. It is important we keep channels of communication open around the world. *Shoreline of Infinity* is our tiny contribution, and we would love to see stories from all parts of the world, and from all cultures.

Any road up, pull up that log, warm your hands by the fire here at the *Shoreline of Infinity*, and as Douglas Adams said: "Share and Enjoy."

Noel Chidwick, Editor-in-Chief,
Shoreline of Infinity.
Edinburgh
December 2015

---

*Painted Ocean is mine and Mark's own band—it was our party, after all.

史剣活

"We Sell Seashells"

Ryan L Daly

Art: Stuart Beel

The Comber, **emblazoned with** the distinctive pink scallop of Aphrodite Offworld, crawled over the dense tan sand, still damp from the shallow tide which receded in the distance. As it moved, its unblinking cameras, mounted in all directions, analysed the surrounding dunes and the grains which composed them. This data augmented the eyes of its human operator, typically bleary and heavy after staring through windows at the alien sands for hours at a time.

Deaf to the ceaseless winds which whipped past the vehicle, Nikola sipped a cup of caffeine-laced liquid which she had been told was coffee. She tapped a button and the rover halted, pelted by grains of sand being borne inland. She looked around, studying the video feeds and windows. Nothing.

She tapped another button and the Comber moved onwards, leaving behind the imprint of its tyres, quickly erased by the weight of the sled following it. This sled was loaded with the objects which Nikola sought on behalf of her employer: seashells. Carried to land by the inflow of currents and powerful tides exerted by the planet's dense moon, these shells sold at auction for a sum that more than justified the expense of obtaining them.

The Comber's computers, of course, didn't know why they were valuable. They knew only to look for a predetermined set of shapes and colours, which it would compare with current market values. Sub-par specimens were ignored, as their reduced size or flawed colours diminished their effects.

Nikola yawned and sipped at the coffee-coloured liquid again, screwing up her face in disgust. The stuff was palatable when hot, but once it had cooled down to room temperature, it was vile. She reached for a thermos and poured some more into the mug, reflecting on the fact that she hadn't seen the bottom of it since starting her work eight months ago. She looked out the windows again. It was growing darker and thus more difficult for her to spot the shells. She leaned back, content to let the computer take over for now.

After another half-hour, as the shadow of the rover grew longer, stretching over the beach, the video-screen to her left beeped and showed a red dot. Searching out the window for it, Nikola spotted the shell. Red, speckled with turquoise discolourations. She'd not seen any like it. Tapping another button on the keyboard, she directed the vehicle towards it, while checking the time. She'd call the day a wrap after this and head for home. Company policy was to only collect shells during the daytime, lest hundreds of thousands of dollars be accidentally crushed by a weary driver.

As the Comber approached the shell, she slowed down, stopping just before it. She stretched her arms, cracked her fingers, and prepared to retrieve it. Controlling the external limbs was an easy process: once she activated the retrieval system, an array of motion-detecting sensors would be activated and then translate the motions of her arms and fingers to those of the mechanical limbs.

This was the part of the operation that required a human touch. For all the robotic capabilities and programming the rover possessed, it simply didn't have the finesse to be able to collect shells in a profitable timeframe. Attempts to speed up the process had resulted only in shattered shells and lost money. For now, Nikola was as much a necessity as the Comber to Aphrodite.

For several minutes she fidgeted with the shell, wiggling it and digging up the sand. It didn't budge. Frustrated, she took a break and glanced at the sun—maybe a half-hour more of sunlight, tops.

She swore and weighed her options. She could leave the shell and come back in the morning, hoping it wouldn't have been covered up by the sand or swept out to sea by the incoming tide. Though the waters here were shallow, the rarified shells floated easily. Her meager finances taunted her.

"Sonuvabitch."

She gulped down the remainder of her drink, finishing the dregs of that first cup, poured months before. She pulled her helmet on, checked the seals, set a timer for twenty minutes, and grabbed a shovel before stepping into the airlock. Precious seconds passed as it depressurised. Nikola tapped her foot and glanced at the timer.

"C'mon!"

Finally, the airlock finished cycling and she stepped out onto the beach. Forgoing her usual surprise at how familiar the sand felt under her boots, she hurried over to the shell and started digging with her hands, carefully but quickly clearing away the area around the base of the shell (or, given its possible size, the top). After making room for the shovel, she inserted its blade into the sand near the shell's surface and pulled it around in a rough circle. Nikola began her excavation.

Excavation, after all, was her true passion. Aphrodite Offworld had recruited her through a university job fair. While the rest of her classmates had dreamed of continuing their archaeological degrees in the mud and grime of the great cities and unknown places of the ancient world, Nikola had grown tired of living from stipend to stipend. She had stopped in front of the Aphrodite booth, plain but for a plastiprint shell lying on a table beside a stack of pamphlets.

A group of her friends walked past and she dipped her head down, hiding her face in intent study of a brochure. Everyone in her course knew it was possible to work for Aphrodite, always on the lookout for steady hands and careful temperaments, in much the same way they knew it was possible to use their degrees to plunder and steal. But, just as there was money in grave-robbing, there was money in becoming a beachcomber.

"You take drugs?"

She looked up, surprised at the question. The company rep, a woman in her late twenties, about five years older than her, repeated the question.

"No. Not shells." She looked around. "I mean, this is a university. No one here can afford them."

The rep nodded. "Good. We don't hire addicts. Not getting high on your own supply and all that. Too messy. You know why they're valuable though?"

Obviously she knew. Everyone knew about shelling out, exposing the iridescent surfaces to ultraviolet light and losing yourself in the vivid colours that danced out, propelling intense emotions and half-formed images into your mind. Aside from the visuals, there was the bonus that, unlike other forms of intoxication, there was no feeling of hangover or comedown. Larger ones, with greater surface area and variety of colours, were more valuable. Some said the effect was a result of the brain being overwhelmed by the rapidity of the shifts between hues and spectrums, while others, usually those who had been users for too long, ascribed the high to some vague intelligence within or beyond the shells.

"Yes. After all, it was the School of Exobiology here that got the first samples." And it was the damn School of Exobiology that got all the funding and glory, at the expense not only of the arts and humanities students, but the other scientific subjects too.

The rep nodded again and smiled. "Well, since you know how valuable they are, I'm sure you'll be delighted to know about the half a percent finders' fee that we offer all our employees."

Two months later, she was learning how to operate a Comber.

After five minutes, she examined what she had uncovered thus far.

This shell really was unlike any she'd seen before. Extraordinary not only in its colours, but in shape and size too. Most were smooth and worn by the washing of the waves, like the mollusks she had collected as a child and as this one had initially appeared. However, as she had dug down, it had begun to look more like a conch, its smoothness breaking up into jagged protuberances, like teeth on a gear, which ran around the surface of the shell about a foot under the sand.

She grinned. Maybe she'd be able to quit and go back to school sooner than she had planned. Eager but still cautious, she pressed her shovel back into the sand, hearing the muted crunch of the granules rubbing against the metal. She lost herself in the steady rhythm of the work. Push down, angle back, lift up, toss aside. Down, back, up, aside.

Eventually, her watch began to beep, but Nikola carried on digging, either ignorant of the sound, dulled as it passed through the thin air and into her helmet, or subconsciously ignoring it, driven by the hope of wealth, and with it, freedom to do as she wished. Freedom to study, freedom to travel, freedom to be a wastrel if she so pleased. Each inch of shell that she exposed was another month's rent, another want, another flurry of numbers in her mind.

As she buried herself in her work the sun set, disappearing from the smooth horizon.

Two hours later Nikola stopped, realising that she could no longer see and risked damaging her prize. She crawled seven feet up the slope of sand, leaving behind the imprints of fingers, knees, and boots. Having reached the rim, she turned on the Comber's lights and surveyed what she had uncovered.

Below the smooth dome of red and blue was the perfectly symmetrical set of twelve spikes, jutting out like horizontal stalactites. These had proven to be the most unusual aspect of the shell—if she could even call it that anymore. Beneath them, the shell had widened out into an equally iridescent cone, the bottom of which she had yet to expose. Unlike normal shells, brittle and unable to take much pressure before shattering, this one appeared to be tough, like chitin. And, unlike other shells, the only part of this one that appeared "normal" was the dome.

Most intriguing was that there seemed to be something inside. A series of gentle raps with her shovel had produced a muffled noise, like tapping on a gumball-filled jar.

Nikola sighed and toyed uneasily with the shovel in her hands, uncertain of what to make of her find. It could be that this was worth a small fortune, or that she had laboured for two hours and circumvented Aphrodite policy only to unearth a worthless bauble, worthy of scientific interest at best. She needed to rest before she could decide what to do.

She sighed again before turning back towards the Comber. Behind her, the moon rose, steadily inching its way above the horizon as she stood in the airlock, awaiting repressurisation. It moved quickly through the sky, dragging the waters of the vast sea with it. By the time that she was back in her seat the moon was fully visible, lighting the beach with an ultraviolet glow, the result of lunar mineral deposits intensifying the sun's rays, the reflection of which interacted with elements and gases in the planetary atmosphere. The shimmering water lapped at the wheels of the rover and trickled down into the pit. Unconcerned, Nikola took a bite from a stale pastry and refilled her coffee mug. Even at high tide, the waters would only be one or two inches at most; there was no risk to her or the shell. She took a sip and paused.

The shell's dome, previously red and blue, now swirled intensely, emitting unnatural combinations of pink, purple, and neon green that roiled back and forth on its surface. She was immediately entranced, unaware that she had dropped her mug to the Comber's floor. Around her, the cabin was filled with kaleidoscopic shadows.

Nikola was lost, literally trapped in a sea of colours. The water that had just been clear and liquid had become vibrant and viscous, no longer splashing upwards as it met the Comber; instead it seemed to crawl up the ridges of the tyres before growing weary and relinquishing its grip, falling. Ebbing and flowing, the tidal current was illuminated by the dome, glimmering like a psychedelic prism and drawing her mind further and further away from herself in a feedback loop of colour and time dilation.

At the edges of her mind, Nikola could feel something else; a sensation that some other mind was searching for a way into hers. Fear took hold and she started struggling, willing her neck to wrench her head away from the pulsating dome or her eyes to shut. Her muscles wouldn't, or couldn't, obey. She tried to swear in frustration, but all that came out of her mouth was a throaty gargle.

Finally, the other made contact, not speaking to her but feeling and emoting at her, projecting experience into her mind. She became it.

He was inching his way out of the sea, leaving behind a trail of mucous as he followed the water. Once it reached high tide and had soaked the sand fully, he began to use the front of his shell to dig into the softness, burrowing down for protection from the dry heat of daytime. Once he was deep enough, he stopped and rested, rehydrating after his exertions.

Then he began to crawl again, this time under the beach, stopping when he encountered a suitable mixture of nutrients and extending one of his twelve ovipositors, now motile and supple. Feeling within the protective armour of his belly he found an egg-shell and deposited it in the moist sands where it would grow, accreting nearby silicon, gravel, and minerals around itself, slowly hardening into a cocoon of nerve fibres and primitive thought. Then he would move onwards, confident that he had chosen a good location where the egg-shell could grow and one day tunnel its way upwards, where the tides that had brought him in would carry the larva-shell out to sea.

From time to time he would encounter others, male and female. He would fight the males, circling around and around his opponent before moving ponderously forwards, using his bulk to force his foe back. Defeated, his rival would leave, relinquishing his grounds. The females, tiny and defenceless, he would woo, inviting them into the safety of his vast body, where their eggs would be guarded and they themselves would be cared for and fed. Even now, in this time of stress, he could feel his mates releasing their eggs to be fertilised and join the countless others that filled his stomach, ready to be released.

When he felt fresh water filter down through the sands, he would move upwards slightly, breaching the surface to speak to his children, sending them calming messages as they waited to be carried out to sea. But now his larva-shells did not lie in the protective embrace of the sand or the sea, but open to the air. He too, was exposed, dug up by this other, his only defence to try and hypnotise it, calm it, so that he could burrow deep and hide…

Punctuating this jumbled mass of imagery was a blast of emotion: confusion and anger mixed with a plea. Why?

The moon set as rapidly as it had risen, snapping Nikola out of her trance as quickly as she had entered it. She was shocked to see that the animal had scooped out the sand around itself, leaving about three feet of its body exposed. Uncertain of what to do, but certain that she needed more time to think, she turned on the external limbs and gouged clumps of moist sand from the ground, tossing them aside, stopping only when she felt confident that the creature couldn't escape without her noticing.

She sat for a time, thinking about her experience of being the beast. He was undoubtedly alive, maybe self-conscious, possibly intelligent. But none of that really mattered. The thing that kept coming back to her was the emotion, particularly the fear, which he had projected into her. She could, in her own way, understand it. Fear of failure, that the desires which drove you would be stopped, could be stopped. The fear that dawned on you as you realised that no matter how large or intelligent you were, there were forces that could exert an even greater power over you and take control of you, twisting you to their own ends and goals.

The darkness of the alien night surrounded her and she shivered, feeling the chill of cooled sweat on her skin and the rush of adrenaline fade into weariness. She sat and thought as the night began to fade away, to be replaced with the faint light of dawn. The creature in the pit dug glacially down, its occasional progress interrupted by the mechanical whirr of the claws. She studied him, pondering the moral and monetary implications of the untold shells contained within him, along with his mates, able to provide a seemingly infinite supply of egg-shells.

The yellow sun rose and Nikola notified Aphrodite.

Citizen Erased

Bethany Ruth Anderson

Art: Harri Conner

His thumb and forefinger pushed at the screen, enlarging the text, bringing it nearer. The subject of the email was "Hello Billy" and he read the line again:

Hello Billy. Just that attachment you were after yesterday. Hope it helps! Frank.

From behind his chair, Billy's wife rested a hand on his shoulder, "Making it bigger isn't going to make it any more real. Are you sure it's not just spam?"

"He signed his name. And it's from his work address—I'm sure security would be on it by now if it was bad." Billy frowned as his hand curled around the mug of coffee his wife had placed in front of him. He tapped again at the attachment. From the Royal Society of Biomedical Research and Experimentation. "I think I want to do it, Naomi. I think we both should."

Her sigh was lost in the clatter of cutlery as she picked it from the dishwasher, "You know I would... But what if something goes wrong?"

Billy sucked coffee between his teeth and picked up the tablet, turning to show his wife, pointing vaguely where he remembered reading it, "We'll get compensation. And they'll fix us right back."

"And if it can't be fixed? I just don't want to walk out of there with my head on backwards or something."

Billy laughed and dabbed at the crumbs on his plate, "That would definitely be fixed. I like your head the way it is."

Naomi sat at the table, picking up a slice of toast as she leaned forward into the small screen between them, "Just promise me one thing."

"What's that?"

"We'll both come out of it alive, and still in love, and we'll both come back here together, just as we are."

"I'm not sure... You're asking me to promise more than one thing, there."

Naomi's eyes rolled away his pedantic sarcasm and she looked at him steadily, "But you're still going to promise?"

"I promise." Billy granted her wish with a small kiss, then brushed crumbs from his chest where he'd leaned over his plate, "Besides, I don't think they're quite clever enough yet to steal all our feelings."

"But you never know," she said. "You never know."

The posters on the wall promoted good health—how to start stopping smoking, where to go if you felt a lump, colourful contraception choices, and anonymous numbers to call in distress. A mother watched her small child beat chair legs with a plastic fire engine. Billy cleared his throat in hopes that the woman might notice that the scrapping noise was upsetting Naomi, who sat wincing beside him. But the mother just stared.

"Mister and Mrs MacKay?" The voice sounded from down a corridor they couldn't see, but they rose together, each clutching a paper bag. They shuffled along the brown carpet until the expectant silence revealed a tall figure in a white coat. The man smiled, and Naomi almost tripped as her shoe slipped from her foot. "If you'd just like to come in and take a seat." Billy reached out to squeeze Naomi's hand, glancing at the pastel green chairs, a shade similar to their kitchen tiles.

"I'm Doctor Dawson, and I'll be guiding you through the procedure today." He continued to smile with practised

reassurance, easing himself into his own leather-backed chair. "Before I begin, do either of you have any questions you'd like to ask?"

Billy glanced at his wife who was twisting the thin paper handles of her bag between her fingers. The car journey had taken them twenty minutes, during which they voiced countless concerns of what-ifs, but surrounded by soft colours and the gentle hum of a fan, they each shook their heads. "No, not that I can think of."

"That's not a problem. Do feel free to intervene with any questions if need be. And at each stage of the process there will be a member of staff on hand to help with any concerns." His shoulders rolled as he relaxed in his chair and smoothed his hands across the desk. Naomi noticed that there were no rings on his fingers. Billy noticed that his hands were particularly smooth and bare. "Now, first is the Relaxation stage. And it is, essentially, just that. You are encouraged to relax, and to focus on the memories you are extracting today. This will be when your Memory Aids are required." He inched forward slightly, eyes flicking to the tops of their paper bags. "We'll then ask you to focus on any sense suited to that memory, and you will be required to taste, or to listen, if necessary."

In Naomi's paper bag was a Tupperware box of her homemade bolognese. Preparing it had been a struggle, both the sight and the smell. She hadn't even tasted it. The lucid flashbacks, flickered through her mind at just the smell of the beef mince and onion. There was no pasta, just the meaty, red sauce.

Billy had started folding his bag, reducing it to the

size of the thin plastic box inside it, to the size of a CD case. Bruce Springsteen. Greatest Hits. He had been lucky that he still had a CD player in the garage, a keepsake from the past. There was a scratch on the mirrored surface of the disc so that the start of Born to Run always skipped, but that was important too.

"Myself, and some members of the cognition team, will be monitoring your memory reflexes. We can only extract the memory when it is of a certain size, and this will be entirely dependent on how well you can focus."

"How long does it usually take?" Billy drummed his fingers on the case on his knee, "For example, if I want to listen to something, and it takes longer to get the memory than the songs lasts."

"There will be someone facilitating the equipment, and we'll ensure that there are no breaks that will disrupt your focus."

"Will it hurt...when you take it out? The extraction, I mean?" Naomi reached into her jacket pocket and pulled out a packet of tissues. The paper bag jiggled on her restless leg as she pulled out a tissue and pressed it against her upper lip, then her forehead.

"Not at all. Strong as memories may seem, they're not actually able to physically cause pain. By the end of the extraction, your memory will be completely gone. We aim to extract the memory of here and now too. When you wake, it will be at the cafe restaurant at the front of the building, just an ordinary place. The feeling has been likened to that of when there's the name of a song that you just can't remember, or when you had something to say but forgot what it was. Quite harmless."

Billy turned to look at Naomi and held out a hand for her, but she was clutching tightly to the Tupperware in her paper bag so he grasped her wrist instead. She made a small whimpering noise but smiled and nodded her head. The doctor smiled back and looked at them both with eyes that promised that he understood.

"Do you have any further questions, or are we happy to carry on?"

"Happy to carry on." The words rushed from Naomi's shaking mouth.

Doctor Dawson bowed his head and pulled open a drawer in his desk. He withdrew two folded pamphlets and slid them across the table. "Recently, we have added another stage to the process. This involves nothing on your part, but it does require permission and will give a small increase to your compensation."

Billy picked up his pamphlet and it quivered in his hand, so he pressed it against the desk with his palms, "Memory Transfusion." The letters were bold silver against a cobalt background.

"That's right. With recent developments, we've also been able to aid research with the artificial intelligence department of the RSBRE. Initially, after Extraction, your memory would become waste. With a Transfusion, the memory can be imported to A.I meaning that it remains, and is available for retrieval, should you need it at any stage. In short, Transfusions will help us both develop A.I and keep your memory alive, as it were. It's really very beneficial to our work here."

Naomi laughed and shook her head, "I'm pretty sure I won't want my memory back. That's why I'm here, after all."

"I understand that, Mrs MacKay, but it is one thing that previous patients have been concerned about in the long-term. Just another option."

"Well, I don't see why not." Billy tucked the wrapped Bruce Springsteen CD into his pocket, then pulled it out again. "I'm happy to do that."

Naomi smiled at her husband, having known that he'd say yes the moment Artificial Intelligence was mentioned. He couldn't refuse helping to develop something that he was so fascinated by, even if he barely understood it.

"Fantastic news, Mr MacKay. We really appreciate your efforts." Doctor Dawson moved excitedly, quickly pulling out a small blue pen from the same drawer. "If you'd just like to read the information, and to sign at the bottom, alongside your signature for the Extraction." He produced another pen for Naomi, but leaned towards Billy, eyes watching for the extra signature. "We will add the extra compensation to your wallet along with the initial payment." The doctor collected the signed papers, added his own flourish, and clipped them to a black clipboard. "Now, are we ready?"

"I just want to thank you so much for doing this for us." Naomi stood too quickly and the chair fell quietly backwards onto the plush carpet. Billy stooped to pick it up and brushed his lips against her cheek.

"You are very welcome, Mrs MacKay, and we thank you for your contributions." He moved around his desk to open the door, motioning with long fingers down the corridor.

Billy linked his arm with Naomi's and they stepped from the room together, his hushed voice at her ear, "Are you okay?"

"I've signed it now."

Coffee. A scent of real, freshly ground coffee. Billy poked at the corners of his eyes before opening them to his wife. She had a laminated menu in her hand, and she smiled at him from the opposite side of the table, "Hi there, sleepy head."

Billy blinked, and his lips moved into a shaky smile, "God, did I doze off?

"Only for a minute. I ordered you a coffee. And some homemade tiffin. It looked delicious."

The cafe was reasonably quiet; just one other couple and a few people sat alone nursing tea and cakes. Music came from the kitchen, bright notes in the major key drifting over the counter.

"Did you still want to pop into the garden centre on the way home?"

"Were we going to?"

"For compost."

A lady approached with a tray, remarkably steady despite the

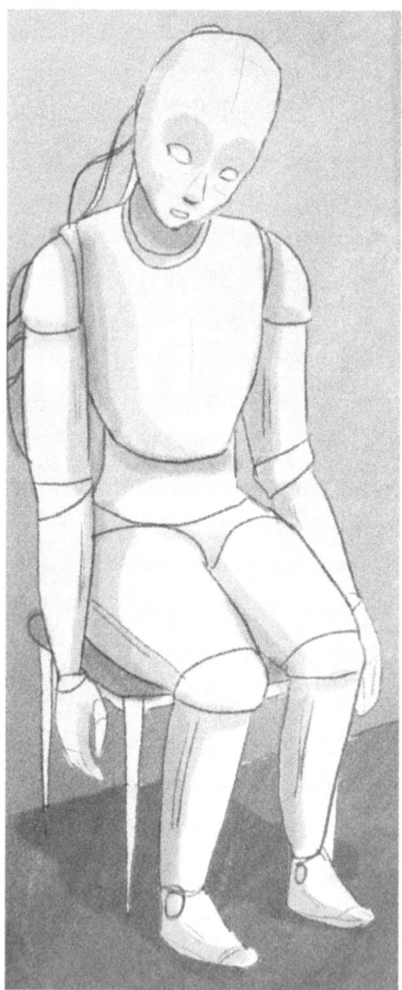

unsure shuffle of her feet. She settled their order onto the red and white gingham cloth, and when she smiled it smoothed the wrinkles round her neck, "There we are. Let me know if there's anything else I can get for you."

Billy smiled at the woman and nodded in thanks before turning back to his wife, "Right. Compost for the plants. That's fine. And we can pick up something for dinner later?"

Naomi stirred a sugar into her tea, tapping the spoon against the cup and being careful not to drip, "I'll make us something. I haven't made my bolognese in a while."

"Sounds good."

They enjoyed their tea and coffee in silence, until Billy suggested that he wanted to try making his own tiffin at home; it couldn't be that hard. Smiling, Naomi gathered up her back and stood to pay the bill, "I'd be more than happy to taste test."

Billy met her at the door and squeezed her hand, kissed her eyebrow, "Do you remember where we parked?"

Outside, there were eight cars neatly parked. "Just over here." Naomi let go of Billy's hand and he searched in his pocket for the keys. "...Billy?"

"Hmm?" He turned to follow her gaze, up and up towards the roof behind them, a building far bigger than the sweet little cafe. It was a small part of a huge factory; the kind of old industrial warehouse that no one seemed to remember ever being in use. Figures walked across the roof in single file, limbs stiff as they marched to the edge. The first paused, took one step, two steps, and fell from the roof. The sound, when it hit the ground, was metal crashing against metal.

Bethany Anderson is an Edinburgh-based writer who enjoys scribbling poetry and prose. She has an MLitt in Creative Writing, and her short stories and poems have been published in various places. Bethany's debut novel *Swings and Roundabouts* explores relationships and mental illness. She is continuing to work on further novels and writes on her blog: www.subtlemelodrama.com. Bethany tweets @subtlemelodrama

Charlie, A Projecting Prestidigitator

Megan Neumann

Art: Dave Alexander

harlie checked his batteries before he went out that night. He didn't want Henderson angry with him again. The night before he hadn't charged completely and only performed three scenes. Henderson hadn't been happy about that. According to Henderson, Charlie wasn't earning his keep. But Charlie would change that soon. He had applied updates to his software that morning. Tonight his images would be more vivid and real.

On the couch, Henderson slept, snoring loudly and occasionally stirring to wheeze and cough. Charlie leaned over and patted Henderson on the head. It was only 8 p.m., but Henderson had drunk too much earlier in the day. The old man would sleep until the early morning hours before checking Charlie's earnings.

Charlie paused before a mirror to polish his silver head with his sleeve. He could hear Henderson's voice in his mind warning, "No one wants to give their money to a filthy pile of junk." Henderson liked to remind Charlie of this. "Look sharp and you'll bring them in." But there were other reasons for cleanliness. The show projected from his face as well as his hands, and any dirt caused artifacts in the images.

When he finished polishing, light gleamed from the top of his head and the point of his chin. He examined his facial features with his optical sensors, searching for remaining smudges or dust. His scan told him he was clean. Charlie smiled at his reflection. "Looking real good, kid," he said in a gruff voice that sounded like Henderson. He chuckled in his own voice, which sounded like robots in old sci-fi movies, stilted and inhuman. Charlie's voice could sound like anything, but Henderson had chosen the robot's voice. Though Henderson never told Charlie why, Charlie suspected the old man liked a reminder of the past.

Stepping outside their basement apartment, Charlie took in the noises of the city. He recorded every sound, analyzing where people congregated nearby, where there was laughter and chatter, where people were having a good time. There were three parks within walking range where people liked to wander on Saturday nights. Couples on dates would sit hand-in-hand on benches and look up at the stars projected onto the sky from building tops.

Henderson preferred Charlie to go to the busiest park first, and then work his way down as the crowd thinned. Charlie found the nearest park was also the busiest. Applegate Gardens was a concrete slab in the center of the city with a few fountains and artificial trees with oxygen producing synthetic leaves. Performers like Charlie put on shows nightly there. He'd compete with these other performers tonight for tips. Henderson had recently upgraded Charlie's speakers, so he'd at least be the loudest performer.

As he made his way toward the park, he sensed a group following him. His rear optical sensors told him it was a crowd of teenagers. They followed him for a block before they said something to him.

"Nice suit, tinman!" one teenager shouted—a young woman. She traveled with six male teenagers. She was the largest of them, and Charlie assumed she was their leader. Charlie knew about gangs in the city. He had dealt with them before.

"Thank you, madam!" he said in his English gentleman's voice. "A good evening to you!"

"You hear that?" one boy said, "you're a 'madam.'"

The teens laughed and followed Charlie, taunting him. "Where you heading in that getup, guy?" one said. "You in the circus?"

Charlie wore something similar to the suits of old circus ringmasters: a bright red, double-breasted jacket with oversized gold buttons and gold fringe hanging from his shoulders.

He didn't respond to any more of their comments. This was how Henderson had trained Charlie to react. Or rather, this was how Henderson had programmed Charlie. Charlie liked to think of his programming as training. He would imagine Henderson spending hours patiently explaining the ways of the world to him. However, much of Charlie's knowledge—Charlie knew—had been downloaded to his hard drives in a few minutes.

Sometimes he wondered how many other Charlies there had been. Once while charging, he had explored Henderson's basement room and found severed limbs and heads similar to his own. This had frightened him, and he had shut down for a few hours. When Charlie rebooted, Henderson had yelled, saying there was no use for a flaky robot. Robots were workers and that was that.

As Charlie recalled this, the girl threw a bottle at his back. It shattered, and his sensors told him he was completely soaked, his jacket most likely stained. Of course, this wasn't the first time someone had thrown something at Charlie. People did that from time to time, and so Henderson inevitably spent many days washing Charlie's suit.

"Whatcha gonna do about that, motherfucker?" the girl yelled. Charlie detected anger in her voice, and he walked faster. Henderson had trained him to avoid angry humans.

"Don't you ignore me!" the girl yelled.

Charlie once asked Henderson why so many people grew angry with robots.

"Usually it's the people who don't have much and who don't know much that hate robots," Henderson had said.

"But you don't have much, and you don't hate me. Do you?"

"No, of course not," Henderson had said, toying with some circuitry in Charlie's back. "But I know quite a bit. And I used to have a lot more than I do now. But I can understand fear of something that could threaten you, even if it's not threatening you at the moment."

Charlie kept these words in mind when dealing with anger and hate. He knew it was not usually anger, only fear.

He continued to the park, and the teens stopped following him, probably growing bored. Humans grew bored quickly. He also kept that in mind during his shows.

A large crowd occupied the park. His olfactory sensors told him vendors around the place were cooking grilled synthetic meats and other savory foods. This pleased Charlie. Humans enjoyed his show more with full stomachs.

In the center of the park, Charlie enabled his upper speakers and said in his best ringmaster's voice, "Ladies and Gentleman, come see a spectacular show unlike any other!" This announcement brought the crowd toward Charlie. "Come see the wonders of the modern world along with the wonders of a world long vanished—a full three-dimensional experience of wonder and joy! Be a child again. Let your imagination soar!"

The crowd made a semi-circle around him. He heard someone whisper, "I've heard of these shows."

Someone else said, "This is lame. Can we go?"

Charlie had heard comments like the latter before, but they still bothered him. Mean comments made something within his skull ache and not want to continue. But his training hid his emotions from his silver face. His training forced him to continue with his show.

He spread his hands outward with his palms flat and facing the crowd. His hands became opaque then glowed; light shone into the night before him. His head glowed too, shining brightly in the center of the half-circle of humans. Shapes and colors projected from his head, and his whole body vibrated, humming with a sound the crowd would not be able to hear over their muttering and their chewing.

The lights changed and the concrete park within the center of the circle vanished. To the crowd, a forest had grown from the ground before their eyes. Charlie used his projection system to define every angle of every tree. Every blade of grass breezing in an artificial wind generated by his chest fans appeared as real as it would have appeared in wild fields long vanished. A small doe grazed silently and seemed as real as any that had once lived on the earth. Charlie heard children in the crowd gasp. A girl ran into the image and tried to touch the doe. Her hand went through the doe's head. The child's father chased after her. He caught her and smiled at the crowd and then at Charlie. The man, catching his unnecessary gesture, blushed in the light of Charlie's forest.

A few birds swooped down and pecked at the ground Charlie had created. The birds, finches and a cardinal, were simple creatures, but no one in this city had ever seen a finch in real life, let alone the bright, scarlet beauty of a cardinal. Charlie projected the sounds of birds chirping from his lower speakers. Some people in the crowd clapped. He heard a few coins landing at his feet. In the crowd, some of his own kind had gathered, service robots finishing their work. The colors and sounds drew them in. Charlie's kind was a curious species, eager to record experiences for later. If they had not trained to project as Charlie had, they would not know of birds or deer. The experience would be new and exciting.

Charlie changed the scene to a vast desert with mountains in the distance. A small fur covered mammal with long, bent legs and a tail emerged from a hole in the ground. A child in the audience exclaimed, "It's cute!" The creature used its back legs to scurry along the desert floor. Then a large bird swooped down and captured the animal in its claws. The same child cried out. Charlie did not like this part of his projection, but Henderson insisted on it.

"You can't hide what the world used to be. Or what it still is," Henderson had said once when Charlie complained.

Charlie heard a few more coins land around his feet. He noticed the crowd dispersing and took that time to dim his projection and lower his hands. "That's all for now, folks," he said, still in his ringmaster's voice. Murmurs of pleasure and annoyance rippled through the crowd. Someone said the show was stupid; someone else said it was a good distraction. That was the best Charlie could hope for from adults—a good distraction.

He kneeled on the hard ground and scooped up the money. He counted it and knew it was less than the night before, and even less than the night before that. His audience declined day by day, even with upgraded software. Henderson wouldn't be happy about this.

Charlie did three more shows that night until his battery indicator started buzzing. He had remaining power to make it home and begin charging before he died.

"Thanks for your attention, ladies and gentlemen," he said as he let the image of a rushing river fade. He heard some protests from the children. They would never feel the cold, wet rushing of a river on their tiny feet. Of course, Charlie would never feel it either.

The noise of the city had quieted since he left his basement apartment. His clock told him it was 1 a.m. On the streets, cars still moved steadily, a constant honking in the distance and nearby. Music played somewhere, coming from an open window. It was the new music Henderson hated—nothing but rhythms and ringing.

Charlie enjoyed all kinds of music. He recorded this so he might listen to it later as he charged. He would replay it over and over and recall the senses from this particular walk.

Something heavy struck Charlie in the head. His body fell forward, his face smashing into the concrete.

"You like that, tinman?" a voice said above him.

Charlie recognized the voice of the female teenager from earlier. She was alone. He didn't sense anyone else around. The female circled him holding something in her hand—a metal bat.

"I'm going to take that shiny head of yours as a prize," she said. Charlie turned his head to face her and record his attack. "You think you can make fun of me? Ignore me? You're nothing. Nothing real."

"I did not mean to offend you, madam," Charlie said, slipping into his gentleman's voice.

"There you go again, making fun of me!" She raised her bat again.

He reached a hand up to shield himself.

"Please," he said in his natural robot's voice. This seemed to startle the girl. She lowered the bat.

"Why?" Charlie asked. Even injured, he wanted an explanation so he might analyze the situation later. Then he processed some thoughts and realized there might not be a later.

The girl stared at him, watching his hand reach toward her. He felt his inner functions activating abnormally. His hand lit up. He projected an image of the girl holding the bat, her projected face a mixture of confusion and fear and hate. This brought the girl back from her stupor. Upon seeing herself, her face twisted in anger again, and she swung the bat in a swift movement. Charlie felt the impact, but could no longer see. Before he shut down, he heard his metal hand clang against the sidewalk.

Charlie awoke unable to detect his legs. An alarm within him told him his batteries were depleted except for his backup solar battery, which was currently charging. His logs showed internal repairs had been made while he was charging.

He sat atop a pile of rubbish, and he was, in fact, part of the rubbish. All around him, he saw nothing but garbage as far as his optical sensors could see. He assumed garbage collectors had swept him up and taken to the dump. Turning his head downward, he saw his legs were smashed. His suit had been stripped from his body, either by the teenaged girl or by some other gang. He hoped Henderson would find him soon.

A remote tracking device in his head should tell Henderson where he was, if Henderson decided to get Charlie. But would he? Henderson was old for a human, Charlie knew. An old man wouldn't be able to move around freely through mountains of garbage.

Then a thought occurred to him—what if Henderson had put Charlie in the dump? Charlie dismissed this quickly because the thought upset his processing. He shut his eyes and charged until he heard a noise beneath him coming from lower in the pile. Charlie opened his eyes. A child stumbled over a large pile of garbage toward Charlie.

"Hello," Charlie said, in his natural, robotic voice. The child, Charlie could not tell if it were male or female, looked at him with obvious curiosity. It did not seem frightened of his silver head or crushed legs. A child living in a garbage heap, Charlie assumed, was accustomed to seeing strange things.

"What's your name?" Charlie asked. He enjoyed the company of children, enjoyed their wonderment when he put on his projections. The child mouthed a word silently, but Charlie read its lips. "Samantha?"

The girl nodded. He sat up, using his elbows to reposition his torso. He leaned his back against a metal drum beside him.

"Well, Samantha, have I got a show for you!" he said in his ringmaster's voice. "Come one, come all! See the wonders of the electronic man!"

The girl's eyes widened. Charlie lit his palms and spread them apart. An alarm warned him there were only two hours of solar battery power remaining. He thought that would be enough to put on a good show.

An image of children playing in a snowy field appeared. The girl gasped. She watched in silence for a moment, and then she grinned. She reached out as though to catch the snowflakes in her hands, though they passed through her.

"What is that?" the girl asked, still attempting to catch the flakes. She stuck her tongue out, mimicking the children in Charlie's projection.

"It's snow," Charlie said, switching back to his robotic voice. "It's something that falls from the sky. A type of precipitation. You would not see it in this part of the world, though it still occurs in northern regions of which you would not be familiar and are uninhabitable for humans."

She nodded as if she understood and watched as he changed to the next scene, the same forest he'd opened with the night before. Another child climbed onto their trash heap and watched with them. This one looked like the girl, only a little older and male. He carried plastic bags full of garbage, but dropped the bags at the sight of the projection. Both children asked questions, timidly at first, then more excitedly as the show went on.

"What animal is this?" the girl asked, pointing at the doe. Then, "What kind of plant is this?" Charlie answered each question as thoroughly as possible, hoping his little knowledge would be enough.

After three scenes, an alarm told him he would need to shut down, his solar battery nearly dead.

"I have to go to sleep now, children," he said.

"When will you wake up?" the girl asked.

"Tomorrow," he said. "Same time, same place."

The boy smiled and said, "We'll be back tomorrow."

Charlie closed his eyes as the children climbed down the heap. He thought of what he would project for them the next day, perhaps schools of fish underwater or elephants or big cats in a jungle. He had thousands of scenes in his hard drives, thousands of images of life to share.

Megan Neumann is a speculative fiction writer living in Little Rock, Arkansas, US. Her stories have appeared in such publications as *Crossed Genres*, *Daily Science Fiction*, and *Luna Station Quarterly*. She is a member of the Central Arkansas Speculative Fiction Writers' Group and is particularly appreciative of their loving support and scathing critiques.

Shoreline of Infinity
Event Horizon

An evening of **science fiction** in Edinburgh
Last Thursday of every month 7.30pm

At Deadhead Comics
30 West Nicolson Street EH8 9DD

Live music
Stories
Films
Drama

Live art
Comics
Poetry
Readings

further information
www.shorelineofinfinity.com/eh

Purgatory

Michael Fontana

Daniel hustled atoms on a street corner in purgatory. The rush was to roll the bones, actual bones, and see if they came up your way to pick up some sweet atoms like to alter your genetic structure. You know what I'm talking about: young atoms, fresh off some new angel's skin, scraped free with an emery board and dropped into the tiniest of plastic bags sealed with a bread tie—for that extra freshness. Daniel hosted pockets full of little plastic bags like this, hectoring the forlorn and listless, rumbling down the streets and alleyways of purgatory.

Purgatory smelled like pickle brine in case you didn't know, just the kind of place you didn't want to land in for too long. The divine order was that you made your way there unbaptized. Maybe some fine young missionary in Namibia or the like would bless the pagan babies so your head was numbered among those summarily blessed, making your move on to heaven or hell as the case and deserving might be.

Daniel stood there a lapsed Catholic. You know the type: insufficient force of will to make and maintain the commitment to the lessons of the rosary. So by faltering he slicked his hair back in Brylcreem, donned his best camo overalls and paint-riddled boots. He began by stomping the thoroughfares with the bones of some sore loser who had shed his skin to make the move onto hell, figuring 24/7 of harps being plucked was like a flipping nightmare rather than a solace.

Anyway I took him up on his gamble, slapping down a fin for a roll of the ulna and losing every time because he had the bones rigged, natch. He had took a paring knife and dug notches in the sides so he could command at what angle the bones would flop when tossed. I was the sucker who hedged his bets because I had nothing else to do down here regardless.

I made my way into purgatory by swiping coins from the offering, on the one hand blessed and sacred in my bedtime prayers, on the other sacrilegious by swiping drops of pablum from the quivering lips of the poor. So I was no salt when it came to Daniel's game. I called him on it. "This is for duffers."

"It's fair and square," he said, slobbering the words like he had a jawful of gobstoppers. He held the bones up to the light and that was where, by squinting, I could see the work of the paring knife on the surfaces.

"Hand me back my fin," I said. I was taller than Daniel, scarlet-bearded, long-haired, glassy eyed and thick of form, unlike him who was a relative twig. I wore my flannel shirt, my jeans, my snakeskin boots and an amulet of a crawdad around my neck for point of emphasis.

"Handing you back nothing," he said and packed up his goods like to hustle off to the next corner.

I wasn't playing that. I took one of the bones and broke it in half, held the sharp edge to his bobbing Adam's apple and waited for the sting of its application to register him to his senses.

"Be cool," he said, wriggling like an albacore inside my arms. "I got the fin right here."

I released him long enough for him to make like he was digging in his pocket. Then he bolted. The little twit was quicker than a starling climbing from a chimney top, down the street and around the corner with my fin still coolly nestled in his front pants pocket.

I followed, but the light was dim and I lost him in the shadows, which in purgatory swam around with electrical impulses in the air like an aquarium full of eels. I reached around in the swamp of the amplified night. I even scattered my hands through a few garbage pails in sodden alleys reeking of urine and eczema, only to come up buck empty.

In time I played the patient game and remained within the alley, eyes peering out for a sign of my nemesis. By daylight he returned to the scene of his hustle like a stick pecking out a familiar melody on a xylophone. He laid out his bones, even the broken one, and made his come-on to the wandering tatters of souls that hung out down that way. "Step right up, buckaroos! Step right up and fill your mitts with raw purgatory gold!"

I stepped up smooth and silently, tapped him on the shoulder and he turned just in time for my fist to make a folding parachute out of his face. He dropped to the ground and I pinned him there, knees on his forearms, the bulk of my bottom on his thighs, grifting around in his pockets in pretzel-like contortions of my arms and hands until I plucked the fin free. Then I stood up and offered him a hand, all gentleman-like, so that he could return to standing as well.

"Why'd you let me up?" He asked.

"Because we're all stuck in this hole they call purgatory. I won't let you rip me off but on the other hand I won't let you lay there like a broken dog waiting for the rumble of the street sweepers. Has to be a better fate than that for even you."

"Ain't no better fate coming for anyone down here, unless they make the prayer list at some come-to-glory parish back on earth. Nobody praying for the likes of me," he said.

"None for me either," I said.

"Then what's to do?"

"Break out them bones again," I said.

He did. I held out the fin. The game began again.

Michael Fontana has just completed his first novel manuscript of speculative fiction. He lives and writes in beautiful Bella Vista, Arkansas.

In this album, we take a journey through life's experiences from daybreak through to eventide. Smooth and mellow themes give a sense of assurance – at times – but there is always a feeling that the unexpected lies around the corner.

Ten-track digital album available now via Bandcamp

thelightdreams.bandcamp.com

bandcamp

World's
Best
Chilli

Death Do Us Part

Tyler Petty

It was **Janine's turn to die**. Her hiking boots skidded down the path's loose gravel, forcing her to scout an alternate route. Shielding her eyes against the sun, she estimated the distance between handholds on a steeper course. It would entail some scrambling, but she could make it. The exhilaration of the jump would be more than worth the effort, and resurrection would invigorate her in time for dinner.

While his wife climbed, Lewis gathered the remnants of their picnic, moved the tiny twigs-and-grass statue she had weaved away from the danger zone, and spread out their new collection tarp. With the old one, missing the target zone had been a legitimate concern, but Janine would have to sprout short-lived wings to miss now. The commercials still trumpeted the helical dangers of missing limbs and genetic extrapolation, although they had never met anyone deformed by a botched resurrection. What had sold them was the all-terrain cart that came with the tarp. Lewis could heft her one-hundred-thirty pound corpse without much trouble, although toting it all the way back to the car would have been tedious. But for Janine to carry his two-hundred-plus pounds of military bulk tomorrow, when it would be his turn to die, was another story.

"Ready?" she shouted from the summit.

Lewis waved the "all clear" toward her silhouette. Janine's outline disappeared as she backed up for a running start, before she reappeared in a spread-eagle dive. Her skin eclipsed the sunlight, transmuting her into a sports bra, shorts, and boots held together by spectral attraction.

When he was the one in the air, the seconds of free fall stretched and collapsed, an hour and an instant at the same time. From the ground, though, terminal acceleration was impossible to gauge. As soon as her feet left the cliff behind, she had already impacted, crashing into the tarp with a force too hurried to be truly impressive.

The blend of canvas and vinyl crinkled underfoot as he inspected her body. She had died on impact, fortunately. Last year, she had survived a wretched landing—limbs mangled, punctured organs leaking, yet somehow clinging to consciousness—forcing him to usher her oblivion. He prayed he would never see such abject agony again.

Lewis surveyed the scene for any stray bits of his wife, but her body had remained within the impact zone. He folded the tarp over her and sealed the edges, then rolled the cart over and set up its vacuum sealer attachment. Removing the air made her less cumbersome.

The nearest resurrection center was down the road from their hotel. After the Wilton Foundation announced their epochal technology, the centers had sprung up seemingly overnight, as if the announcement were not a serendipitous leap forward, but the latter stages of a meticulous reshaping of the world's economy.

When they drove to the cliff that morning, they had passed a diner boasting the Best Chili in the World. On his way back, Lewis pulled in and strolled up to the counter, leaving Janine's corpse in the trunk.

"What'll it be?" asked the waitress, a middle-aged redhead whose smile said she worked here by choice, not out of necessity.

"That chili sign caught my eye while I was driving past. I consider myself something of an expert," Lewis replied. "I'm pretty thirsty, too. What kinds of beer do you have?"

"Just the one." She nodded at the logo behind her. "Will that work for you?" He nodded in return. "Be back in a minute, hon."

The diner had a carefully curated atmosphere, steps above a dive but too coarse for a franchise. Photographs of the area's countryside and wildlife populated the walls, with truckers' hats advertising companies Lewis had never heard of. The waitress set a steaming bowl of chili in front of him, then grabbed a beer from the cooler. She uncapped it against the edge of the counter and slid it beside the bowl.

"Let me know if you'd like anything else," she said, leaving to attend to a family that had slid into a booth. The husband and wife sat together on one side, their son by himself on the other. The boy's legs reached halfway to the floor.

"The white chili's even better."

Lewis swiveled toward the voice, his knee rebounding off the speaker's hip, and he drifted back to face his bowl.

"Whoa, didn't mean to freak you out. You all right?"

The voice belonged to a tall woman with wavy brown hair and turquoise eyes. She wore a loose sundress and sandals with leather straps that bisected her ankles and lower calves.

"What? Yeah, I'm fine."

"I'm Mills, by the way. It's short for Mildred," she added, "which is an old lady name, so once I wasn't an old lady anymore, I had to shorten it. 'Millie' is old lady, too."

"Yeah, lots of people roll back their age."

"I was one of the first volunteers. My husband died a few months before the machines, and once Wilton decided people like him wouldn't be coming back, I didn't know what to do with myself. "

"You must have been desperate, if 'Wilton guinea pig' sounded like a good option."

She smirked. "Our kids were already grown. Wilton and I both knew no one would miss me if it went sideways. And I had my husband waiting for me if it did. Now I'm a photographer." She looked at the pictures on the wall. "Not just for this place, of course, but these are some of my favorites. The light around here is terrific. What about you?"

Lewis swallowed a mouthful of chili and took a pull from his beer before answering. "I'm just on vacation. Leave, technically. I'm a peacekeeper for Wilton. I'll start my new deployment in a few weeks. Can't say where. Half of what Wilton does is classified. In fact, I might have to take you in just for saying that. You know too much now."

Mills gave him a conspiratorial pat on the wrist. "I had to sign a Wilton NDA of my own. I know how scary their lawyers can be. So, how long are you in town?"

"A few more days." At the glint in Mills's eyes, the tenor of their conversation finally dawned on him. He spooned chili to buy time. "But I'm going to be pretty busy. I have dinner plans tonight."

"Well, if your schedule opens up, feel free to give me a call." She slid a business card out of her bag and into his shorts pocket. "I'll be shooting the rocks for the next day or two. It gets lonely out there."

While the waitress took Mills' order, Lewis shoveled the rest of his chili. He thought better of chugging the beer and hurried out to the car, chuckling at the story he would tell Janine after she was resurrected.

Sunlight streamed through the window, dazzling Janine when she opened her eyes. She groped across the resurrection room for her clothes, finally finding them on the table in the corner, where they always were. It took a minute for her memory to catch up to her body. While she dressed, Janine glanced at the clock above the machine that had just reconstituted and vivified her. The clock was fast. It had to be. She should have come back half an hour ago.

Her spongy flip-flops exhaled against her feet. In the hall, Janine found a resurrection tech and told him about the clock. He returned a moment later, looking concerned. "Are you feeling all right, ma'am?" he asked. "Time distortion is an occasional side effect of the process."

"I know the side effects. This isn't my first resurrection," she replied, more brusque than she had intended. "It's just, that clock's off, right?"

"No, it's right on time. But like I said, some people experience missing time." He checked her delivery record on a screen by the door. "You were brought in complete, so we didn't have to synthesize anything. I could still run a diagnostic, just in case."

"I don't need a diagnostic." She sidestepped the tech and stumbled out to the lobby, where Lewis was folding their industrially dry-cleaned tarp.

"Let me see your watch, or phone. Whatever. Something with the time on it."

Lewis pulled his phone out of his pocket and Mills's business card fluttered to the floor. Janine scrutinized the screen while he retrieved the card. "Your phone is wrong, too," she said. "What the hell is going on? All the clocks are fast."

Lewis pocketed the card. "Let's go back to the hotel. I'll explain about the time on the way."

He finished the story while they were walking past the concierge desk, but she waited until they were in the elevator to respond. "What the fuck, Lewis?" she yelled at the control panel, unable to face him.

"What? You heard me, right? Nothing happened. I left as soon as I figured out she was hitting on me."

"Do you really think that's the issue?" she asked, steadying herself on the arm rail.

"Then what is it? Sorry, but I don't get why you're so mad."

"Alright, let's review." She turned, her gray eyes staring through him. She absently rubbed her shoulder, sliding the strap of her tank top along her shoulder blade. "I died, and your first thought was, 'Hey, chili sounds good.' Did I miss anything?"

Lewis shook his head. "That's not what it was like. I mean, we both saw the sign this morning."

"And at any point—while my corpse was in the trunk, remember—did you think about, I don't know, waiting until I was alive again and going back with me? So we could try the best chili in the goddamn world together?"

The elevator stopped at their floor. Lewis followed Janine out. "Okay, I get it now. I didn't think about it like that. I wasn't thinking at all, to be honest. It just happened. I mean, you were dead. What's the big deal?"

She stopped in front of their room. After a passing maid was out of earshot, Janine asked, "Were we still married? You in the diner with sexy picture girl, me wrapped up in the trunk. Was I your still wife?" She felt her pockets for a wallet or the room key, forgetting she had entrusted her possessions to him before the jump. "Open the damn door."

"First of all, I never called her sexy. I said she was pretty, but that's different." He followed her into the room. "And yes, of course we were still married. As soon as I left the diner, my first thought was how I'd tell you about it. Although I imagined it would go better than this."

"What about deployments? Are we still married then?"

"Do I really need to answer that?"

"And did telling this photographer about my art even occur to you? You know, the sculptures your wife creates while you're on the other side of the world?" Janine flopped onto the chair by the window. "That's what I thought. I need to not look at you for a while."

"Okay if I take a shower?"

"Fine."

He peeled off his dusty T-shirt and shorts, tossed them on the bed, and went into the bathroom. The shower started a minute later. He left his dirty clothes where they were going to sleep, assuming they could stand to spend the night in the same room. Janine slipped off her flip-flops and kicked Lewis' clothes to the floor, sending a small paper rectangle fluttering after them.

"That grandmotherfucker," she said, scanning Mills' business card.

Janine ransacked the suitcase for her hair straightener. Its serpentine cord trailed as she carried it into the bathroom. Before her husband could react to the intrusion, she plugged it in and tossed it under the shower curtain. She teased her hair in the mirror while he sputtered. After unplugging the cord and waiting for any residual charge to dissipate, she turned off the water and went back to the main room. She stretched her legs on the bed and turned on the TV.

It was the middle of the afternoon, so nothing good was on. She flipped between an ambush talk show and a volleyball match. At the top of the hour, she dialed the front desk from the nightstand phone, choked up some tears, and said, "Uh, there was an accident…Yeah, in my room. My husband was taking a shower and, and I was doing my hair, but I slipped. The straightener, it…yeah. Yes, yes I do. He's a big guy."

The eastern sun glanced off the windshield. Janine, wearing running tights and a zip-up fleece, tried to hip check her track-suited husband away from the driver's door. He caught her when she rebounded off him.

"Might as well give me your keys now," she said.

"Oh, right." With an exaggerated twitch, he fished them out of his pocket, adding his wallet and a granola bar he had swiped from the continental breakfast to her supplicant hands.

"It's my turn."

Tyler J. Petty earned an MA in Creative Writing from Ball State University in 2012. His stories have appeared in *The Rag, Oblong,* and *The Broken Plate,* and he is currently working on other stories and novels set in the Resurrection Machine world.
He lives and teaches in northern Indiana.
Twitter: @tylerjpetty

Reliquaries

Steve Simpson

Art: Mark Toner

They pulled at his clothes, exhorted him to pray or donate or confess, to believe or disbelieve. Sunday's spiritual market was meddlesome and curious, but Eduardo knew it was where he would find Joana.

He'd woken to an empty space beside him in the bed, with an empty hollow in the pit of his stomach, and known immediately. It was far from the first time.

The market had appeared in Curitiba at the end of the Superior War, the war that had broken the wheel of the world. By day the northern winds carried dust from Brazil's ruined cities, and at night a band of shattered moonlets shone down on the tideless Atlantic. No-one denied that humanity's end was near, and the desperate search for meaning never ceased. The market was always busy, filled with seekers of salvation who explored the patchwork of cults and churches and solicited snippets of truth from hippie hedonists and sombre embracers of the emptiness to come.

He made his way through the crowds to the Dada pulpit. The Dada acolytes wore no robes, and never preached to their random congregation. Anyone was welcome to take the microphone, and anyone did.

"The goddess has come to the end of time to save us. We must go to her. Each must bring her an offering."

"Oh man, she's *louca*, completely crazy." The stranger stood beside him at the front of the sparse audience. He wore tennis shorts and carried a knife. "I like her pyjamas though."

"They were a gift. I gave them to her on our wedding anniversary."

"I'm sorry, amigo, I didn't—"

He shrugged, "I'm glad you like them, senhor," and he called out to Joana, "Come home, darling. They're only here to laugh and ridicule you."

He looked towards the assembly of the curious and the bored, the glazed eyes that now were more intrigued with the prospect of a squabble.

"I must go, my faithful followers, but please remember my words. When you hear her voice, obey."

She left the pulpit, and he didn't chastise her, but she saw the look in his eyes.

"I'm sorry amor. If I'd woken you, you would have tried to stop me."

The tennis player was next in line to speak.

"We have all lost, game, set and match." He held up the knife. "Who will join me in the world to come?"

She served the pasta and he could almost see them, clinging to her tight curls like damp seaweed—the incomprehensible longings, the whispers that only she could hear. It was getting worse, and Joana asked him over and again to come with her, to accompany her to the Basin where the goddess waited, because that was the pilgrimage her deity demanded.

There was no time off that evening, and he hadn't expected there would be.

"I understand how important this is to you, darling, but the Basin isn't safe. I know the rumours can't all be true, but they say that anyone who comes back is changed, they're hardly human."

The land of the Basin had subsided suddenly, for no apparent reason, as if some ancient and over-sized god had trodden in Paraná and left a footprint. Before its fall, the region had been farms and forests, dotted with a few small towns. Most of the dwellings collapsed with the earthquake of the sinking, but that wasn't the end of it for the survivors.

In the aftermath, people disappeared or were found dead with no apparent cause, and then the rumours started—a secret military weapon had gone wrong, or the devil had marked the Basin for his own, or the war's nuclear bombing, like a lighthouse beacon, had attracted something from the voids of space. Or all of the above.

But whatever you chose to believe, the sunken land was a place of evil, and it really didn't matter why.

"Please, amor. We will plan and travel carefully." Joana looked at him with big green eyes and added the clincher, "The voices will leave me then. I'm sure of it."

That Joana's torments would cease weighed against the unknown horrors of the Basin. Fearful possibilities and probabilities that Eduardo couldn't resolve, and he put off deciding. He always put off deciding.

"Let's think about it, darling. Just for a little longer."

On Monday morning in bed Joana was listless and squirming, pressed against Eduardo's body. She stared out the window facing west when he climaxed.

When he came home from work in the evening, he found a message on the kitchen table. It said not to follow her, that she would return, and on Thursday could he please remember to put the garbage out?

It was two days' wait for the next electric train, and three days west along the Via de Ferro to Gateway Town.

The carriages rattled and shook up the serra beyond Guarapava. In the plains, they wound round craters where the nuclear infernos of the war had fired the clay to ceramic and tracks couldn't safely be bedded. On the final evening of the journey, the rebuilt hydroelectrics on the Iguaçu River failed, and like a weary traveller, the train rolled to rest in the pine forests outside Laranjeiras. Eduardo had time for regrets.

Joana had never kept her affliction a secret, at least not from him. The calling had strengthened in six months to the verge of being irresistible, yet he'd done nothing.

And Joana wasn't the only one. Some said that those affected had been born with an unwanted gift—a bioweapon engineered during the war, a recessive gene for telepathy that skipped generations then reappeared. Whatever its origin, Eduardo knew of others who had already succumbed and left Curitiba for the Basin. Yet he'd done nothing.

The train's electric lights flickered and the loudspeakers advised passengers to reboard for immediate departure.

They should have faced the Basin together, but Eduardo had left it too late.

Joana made slow progress along the old road to Santa Helena. The bitumen had crazed and tilted, folded itself into unlikely obstacles, and she had to pick her way through. But she knew that before nightfall she'd reach the heart of the Basin, and her longed-for destination.

Other pilgrims, muscular men who carried impressive offerings, overtook her, greeting her as they passed because they were all bound for the same holy place. They carried building material and technology, and one even had a dishwasher on his back.

Her burden was barely ten kilograms of reinforced concrete, but its rough surface had ground the skin from her hands, left weeping cuts and callouses. It was her penance, the price for her redemption, and she accepted it gladly.

"Senhora, senhora, please." A young girl had come up beside her on the road, and Joana stopped to talk with her.

"My mother told me not to go outside, but she's very sick."

"Your house is somewhere close, darling?"

"It's just beyond that rise."

"I thought that no-one lived here anymore."

"Mamãe told me we would never leave, that our home was blessed and we were safe. Now every day she tells me to stay inside, and she never gets out of her bed. There's nothing to eat."

Joana hesitated. The insistent voice of the goddess sang in her head—a diversion was out of the question, she must continue her pilgrimage.

"I've asked everyone, no-one will help me. You're the only one who's even stopped."

She looked at the girl's bare feet, her torn jeans, her brown eyes that had nothing to hide, and with the goddess still calling her, Joana reached for her humanity and found it.

She accompanied the girl to the farmhouse.

"Mamãe says the same thing all the time, Don't go outside, Bring me water and sweets, and she never gets out of bed. It smells terrible in there." Marisinha lowered her voice for the last comment, as she'd heard adults do.

Joana entered the bedroom and greeted Marisinha's mother, who was sitting upright in the bed. She seemed to be unaware of Joana's presence and made no reply. Her skin was pallid and sickly, and her head moved in small jerks, with her gaze fixing on random points. Eventually she said, Don't go outside, but her advice was directed to no-one in particular.

Joana approached the poor woman, who still ignored her, and noticed a trail of bone-colored ants scurrying down the wooden bedhead and up into her ear. The ants carried tiny larvae in their mandibles.

Instinctively she brushed them aside and disrupted their path. After a few moments, the woman's jerking movements stopped, her eyes closed, and she tumbled over sideways.

Joana felt for a pulse, but there was nothing, and her flesh was cold. Marisinha's mother had been dead for a long time, but the insects that infested her body had somehow held it in an imitation of life.

"What's happened to mamãe?"

Marisinha was waiting at the door. Joana took her hand and led her away.

"I'm sorry, my love. Nothing can be done for your mother. She's with the Holy Father now."

She held the girl as she sobbed, and promised that she would look after her from now on.

Eduardo decided to overnight in a Gateway Town hotel before he set out the following morning, and after he'd eaten, he decided to pay a visit to a nearby church.

The church was generic, with abstract religious iconography decorating the walls, and Eduardo petitioned any god who would listen to keep Joana safe.

After a little searching, he found the padre napping behind the altar and woke him up.

"I must leave at first light tomorrow, Father, and journey to the heart of the Basin. Will you give me a blessing to protect me from the evil of that place?"

The good man offered Eduardo a quartz talisman that he claimed would keep a traveller safe, but the price was more than Eduardo could afford, and he thought he could see traces of dry blood when the padre turned the trinket in the light.

Afterwards he strolled along the dismal downtown thoroughfares, past the rag doll prostitutes and their clients—the soldiers garrisoned in Gateway Town whose pockets were deep enough to pay—and went to the gateway itself.

For almost an hour he waited by the wooden arch, hoping to see a traveller return, and for some confirmation, however slight, that Joana might still be rescued.

Eventually a bedraggled figure came through the arch, with patches of dark blood spotting his torn clothes. The soldiers who stood guard at the gate asked to see his documents, but he walked past in silence, with his eyes fixed on some unknowable destination and his mouth locked in a frozen grimace.

When the stranger reached Eduardo, he questioned him as well.

"Good evening, senhor, perhaps you can help me," he said, and described Joana, pleaded for any scrap of news.

The stranger looked towards him, and opened his mouth with trickles of saliva. There was a chitinous tongue inside, and waving segmented legs.

Without speaking a word the stranger continued on his way, and the guards who'd been quietly debating reached a decision. A shot rang out, and he fell dead in the street.

In the morning Eduardo set off. He passed beneath the wooden arch and headed down the walkway suspended above the cliffs that marked the Basin's edge.

There were other travellers behind and in front of him, and they carried haphazard objects in their hands or strapped on their backs. Like Joana, they'd been summoned by the goddess in the sunken land.

Joana reversed her steps and travelled back to the south, towards Gateway Town, taking Marisinha to safety as she'd promised.

She didn't cross paths with Eduardo, and after a day's journey, they reached the swaying walkway leading out of the Basin. The number of pilgrims travelling to the pyramid had increased, and the descending crowd slowed them. They stared at Joana, and some called her heretic and heathen.

They might have reached safety, crossed beneath the archway just up ahead, but a single minded volition rose from the press of the faithful all around them, and the reinforced call of the goddess swept Joanna away like a moth in a hurricane.

"Go into the town, Marisinha. I have to go back, I'm sorry. Go to my husband, Eduardo," and she wrote his address on a slip of paper, unsteadily as the pathway shuddered under the tread of the disciples.

"No. I want to come with you," Marisinha said, "But I have nothing to bring her."

A passing pilgrim with a sack of masonry overheard. "Here. Something for you, and you," and he handed each of them a broken tile.

Joana thanked him, and they turned back from the gateway to travel northward again.

The same fluting song began in Eduardo's head, and grew stronger as he approached the centre of the Basin. It rasped away his willpower, and when the pilgrims' destination was in sight, a roughly built pyramid of rubble outside the remains of Santa Helena, he was ready to join them, to travel with them. In the distance he could see them clambering ant-like up the pyramid's sides, and vanishing from sight at the apex where they descended to the goddess within.

He knew that if he continued along the road, she would direct all of his thoughts, and he'd be unable to help Joana even if he found her. He made an effort to take his eyes off the pyramid and look around, and with his feet still carrying him onward like a somnambulist, he tried to change his course.

On a nearby rise, he saw a building with cracked stucco walls and broken terracotta roof tiles. It stood beside a forlorn parking area sprouting weeds, with a sign that stuttered 'Museu Museo Museum.'

He forced his legs to march away from the procession, and step by dogged step he made his way up to the museum.

There was an improbable attendant waiting at the entrance, and as he rummaged through his pockets for a coin, the attendant smiled. "Entry is free today, senhor."

Eduardo wondered how business was going, but didn't enquire.

To distract himself from the sing-song call of the goddess, he wandered from room to room, and the attendant followed shuffling, sometimes offering commentary on the exhibits. There were dusty cases with pinned butterflies and beetles, horns and tusks, and large bristled creatures that resembled dried out thistles.

"Magamalabares," the attendant informed him, as if he should have known what that meant.

Eduardo came to a doorway labelled 'Hallway of Heroes,' and the attendant straightened his back. "This is the centrepiece of our little museum."

They passed slowly side by side down the corridor, with heroes to the left and right looking down on them. Some were missing limbs, and some were simply body parts on pedestals. Eduardo didn't recognize any of the names on the plaques, they were all John Smith or Fulana De Tal, but he didn't ask.

Near the end of the corridor, they came to a wizened figure dressed in an oversize pinstripe suit, held upright by a steel rod running to the floor.

"Before the war, my father was curator. He looks good doesn't he?" The attendant lowered his voice, as if his words might echo in the dried-out ears of the heroes. "I applied a little makeup."

Adjacent to the curator stood an empty pedestal labelled 'Museum Attendant,' but the attendant made no comment.

After that, they inspected a few more mummified and incomplete heroes, and the tour was done. The attendant spoke by rote. "It gives me great pleasure to offer you a complimentary beverage in the museum coffee shop, which always proves a favourite with our visitors."

The attendant boiled water on a kerosene stove, and served him tea with the dry smell of dust and ashes, a bitter reminder of times long past.

"I hope you will return to our establishment in the future, senhor, and I'm wondering whether you would consider making a small donation to support us."

"What did you have in mind?"

The attendant produced a pair of pliers from his pocket. "An unwanted body part—a tooth, or perhaps a fingernail. To fill the displays."

"I may have something suitable. But first, might I ask some questions?"

The attendant agreed, and put the pliers away.

"I haven't noticed any other visitors to your establishment."

"Before the land fell, there were tourist buses every day. Whole families sat at these tables sipping cappuccinos and nibbling sweets." The attendant's small red eyes were becoming misty. "You are the second visitor this year. No-one stops at the museum now, they're all on their way to the pyramid."

Eduardo nodded. The goddess was still insisting that he join the penitential procession, but in the presence of the attendant, Eduardo's thoughts crawled like slugs through his brain, and the edge of her screeching summons was dulled, wrapped in a blanket of futility.

"And you senhor, you do not wish to join them? How do you survive so close by her kingdom?"

The attendant sighed. "... I suppose I may tell you. Many voices sound in the void of my thoughts, but my father's dying wish was that I should care for the museum. His instruction dominates all the others."

"You said I was the second visitor."

The attendant gestured towards a shadowed corner of the coffee shop. "He turned up last week."

Eduardo went over to the unmoving figure, a frail-looking old man sitting in front of half a cup of cold tea, with a chromed walking stick rested against the table. His eyes were closed, but there was a patch of urine on his pants that still looked damp.

"How long has he been like this?"

"A day or two. When I'm sure he's dead I'll put his body on display." He mused out loud. "Mummified of course, and perhaps a little rouge to flush his cheeks."

There was a piece of paper pinned to the stranger's sunken chest. It read 'Por favor, press me,' with an arrow drawn towards a button on the stranger's backpack.

"Did you follow this instruction?" Eduardo asked.

"Was I to press the button? I am not Alícia, and this is not Wonderland, senhor."

Although he'd tried to push the thought away, Eduardo knew it was too late for Joana. She must have long since been swallowed by the pyramid. But the being who called from within it might still

be stopped, and for that, he would need help.

Eduardo pressed the button.

The old man's body lurched violently, he fell to the ground and let out a scream. Eduardo noticed metal disks above the stranger's ears, with insulated wires running to the backpack.

After a few seconds, the screaming stopped and the old man pulled himself up, holding on to the table. "Thank you, senhor," he croaked and panted, "You saved my life."

The attendant brought a fresh cup of tea and the stranger gulped it down gratefully, with a little coughing and regurgitation.

He introduced himself as Silenio and answered Eduardo's questions. "I am a jitter. Do you know what that is?"

"I do, but I thought that no-one …"

They'd appeared at the peak of the war's atrocities—antennae trailed by drones that emitted signals tuned to the brain's oscillations. Any human mind in the range of the radiation was affected with uncontrolled growth of synaptic links, and accelerating confusion and madness.

The name came from the early signs, the jittery movements, the inability to raise a cup to the lips because their intentions were always changing. After that, they became one of Rodin's Penseurs, trapped within themselves, thinking on anything and everything. Their mental train switched tracks continuously, and any practical objective was lost, left behind in a second.

"Survived?" The stranger shrugged. "Perhaps death would have been better than this. But I was a munitions expert—they needed me, and they found an answer."

He pointed at his temples. "Electric shock to the frontal lobes of the brain. It acts as a reset, and I have an hour before it starts again. The automatic timer in my backpack must have failed. I always wear the sign, so that some kind passer-by might assist me.

"I appear to have been in this coffee shop for some time." Silenio glared at the attendant. "I should be able to repair the device with suitable parts. Senhor, might there be some disused electronics in your museum?"

"Of course. My father collected memorabilia from the war that I haven't had time to sort and put on display. The materiel is stored in the horticultural hothouse."

The attendant, no doubt disappointed that Silenio's body would not be added to his collection, thought for a moment. "I must still request a memento for the museum. A significant body part would be appropriate."

Silenio, also thoughtful, nodded.

The hothouse was just a steel frame with protruding shards of glass, and the interior consisted of weeds and a variety of tropical plants and creepers that had grown wild over piles of rusted parts. There was military equipment of every description, some of it blackened and melted. Silenio pointed out a piece of unexploded ordinance, and Eduardo waited with the attendant while he rummaged through the bric-a-brac, scattering it with his walking stick.

"If I might ask, Senhor Silenio, what brought you to this place?"

"I've grown weary of my life, its constant stops and painful starts. After I heard a sermon from an insightful tennis player at Curitiba's spiritual fair, I decided to put an end to it. I came to the Basin out of curiosity, to see what all the fuss was about before I moved on."

"And you don't hear the song of the goddess? You're not compelled to go to her?"

"Like the pilgrims on the road outside? Apparently my condition has given me some form of immunity. And what about you, Eduardo? Why have you come to the Basin?"

Eduardo told them about Joana, and that he knew it was too late to save her.

"But we can help the others who are travelling to the pyramid. We can work together, somehow stop this goddess who controls them like puppets. You are both immune to her calling."

"I have to care for the museum every day. I cannot leave, senhor." The attendant spoke with surprise, as if this should have been obvious to Eduardo.

Silenio hesitated. "It's worth considering. I'm not sure what we could do. I can't walk very well." He scratched the stubble on his chin. "Climbing the pyramid might prove difficult. We have to consider the pilgrims' rights." He stopped scratching. "Entering the mound is what they want. This life has little to offer, perhaps there is a better one within." He started scratching again. "I'll have to think further on the situation."

Eduardo realized that Silenio wasn't free from his affliction—his inability to decide on a course of action—even between his bouts of electroshock therapy. And he knew that he'd lost Joana because of his own indecision.

Now his guilt and grief turned to anger. "Something has to be done, and if you two cowards won't help me, I'll do it by myself."

Eduardo stormed out of the hothouse.

"This might do the trick," Silenio held up a piece of electronics trailing a tangle of coloured wires, "If you have some tools."

"Let's go to my workshop, " the attendant replied, "It's fully equipped, and I even stock a set of surgical instruments for museum supporters who choose to donate a redundant internal organ."

"Thank you for the suggestion, senhor. I'll certainly consider it, but a soldering iron and a pair of pliers will suffice for now."

Eduardo returned to the coffee shop and prepared himself another cup of dusty tea. He paced back and forth with his thoughts in a turmoil, wondering what to do and how to do it.

Without the aura of the attendant to protect him, the piping melody of the goddess took hold of him suddenly and completely, and he no longer had to choose his course of action.

The queue was single file near the lip of the pyramid and it moved forward slowly, fuelling Eduardo's impatience.

Silhouetted against the Andes in the north, he could see a great wreck on the plain, blackened and twisted metal, an unearthly craft that must have come to Paraná from the depths of space, or from some incomprehensible dimension. It was of little interest to Eduardo, and he returned his attention to the line of pilgrims in front of him.

He felt a sharp rap against his shins and turned to see Silenio, the old jitter from the museum.

"Senhor Eduardo, would you be so kind as to make a space for me in the queue?"

"I'm glad you've seen the light, Silenio, but you have to go back to the start of the line and wait your turn." He pushed him roughly away.

The disciples behind Eduardo added their commentary, "Get lost, old man, go to hell."

Silenio sighed. "That's what I thought."

He held up his gift, a piece of wartime junk. "You wouldn't like to swap would you? This is hard for me to manage with the walking stick."

Eduardo compared the dented kettle he'd taken from the coffee shop with the imposing contraption that Silenio held out, and agreed to the exchange.

In the anteroom of the pyramid, the pilgrims were met by metal skeletons, animated by oily cords wrapped over pulleys and levered gimbal joints. They paused the queue so that the penitents passed one by one through a doorway at the end of the chamber. There was a copper welcome mat on the cobbled floor beneath it, and a fringe of wires draping from above brushed on their heads and shoulders as they went through.

When they trod on the mat, there was a bang, and pulses of electricity surged from the wires and through their bodies. Eduardo saw the hair of each disciple stand on end with flashes of bright corona, and smelt the tang of ozone in the air.

Their bodies shook and stuttered with sizzling sounds, but they didn't fall. They staggered onward with vibrating limbs to whatever lay beyond.

Eduardo felt a twinge of anxiety when his turn came, but the goddess soothed him, assured him everything would be fine.

❖

In the main hall, the new arrivals stood in line, with tremors rippling through their bodies as if earthquakes had begun inside them. When their flesh cracked open, their blood and bodily fluids didn't pool beneath them, but coalesced into living creatures, russet serpents that slithered to drain holes and downward to the sub-terrain, where they would serve at the pleasure of the unearthly goddess below.

Hybrid men gathered around each disintegrating figure. Some took their gifts in shopping carts, and wheeled them to a lower level where they placed them in various aisles in the pyramid's department store. One carried Eduardo's gift to a row displaying microwave ovens, mobile phones, and cartoon clocks taken from children.

Up above, other metal-and-meat hybrids worked on the bodies, plucking off flesh and tendons, muscles and nerves. They turned each wriggling piece in their hands and made selections. Some they pushed into crevices in their own chaotic forms, for personal integration, and others were discarded to writhe helplessly at their feet, until pale bats that were circling above flew down to fight over the morsels.

Even when the pilgrims' remains were no more than bloodied bones, their skeletons quivered on the ground until they bent and snapped and reformed into a myriad of insects—scuttling ants and beetles, and dragonflies with splintered wings.

❖

The attendant had told Silenio that he was strongly attached to the museum's kettle, and he'd agreed to retrieve it. He was halfway down the side of the pyramid with the kettle in his hand when he started to reminisce.

He thought of his childhood in Cubatão before the war, the crisp morning air, long socks, trucks on the Via Anchieta, a florist shop, chrysanthemums, graves, his dear wife Julieta, her lips and gestures and knitting, socks again, and on and on.

Silenio's recollections rose with little rhyme and no reason. He stopped walking and sat down on a concrete slab, with endless bubbles of thought fizzing in his head. The timer in Silenio's backpack might have delivered the shock to his temples that would have reset his thoughts and allowed him to act. But another clock was counting down, and it reached zero first.

It was the timer in the compact nuclear device he'd given to Eduardo in exchange for the kettle.

A blue flame shot from the mouth of the pyramid, not with volcanic fire, but like an immense high pressure gas jet. A moment later, a deep rumbling came from below and the mound collapsed inward and downward on itself, carrying Silenio with it.

From the car park, the museum attendant watched the pillar of dust and smoke rise to block the sun. He wouldn't be getting his kettle back, he was sure of that, but the procession of pilgrims to the now-collapsed pyramid was stopping. They put down the items they'd carried on their long journeys and looked around, wondering what to do next. The attendant seized the moment—it was a chance to acquire a few more body parts at the very least— and he found a tattered banner to hang on the wall outside.

It read 'Museum Open, Familial Discounts,' and on the roadway below, he saw a young girl point and pull at a woman's hand.

The attendant accompanied the woman and child in the Hallway of Heroes, and they stopped before the most recent addition, a poorly crafted ring, an unsatisfactory item he'd reluctantly accepted from Eduardo.

The attendant had devised the plan with Silenio. He was certain that Eduardo had taken the explosive into the pyramid, and he told the visitors the story.

The woman snatched up the ring before he could stop her. She turned it over in her hands, and seemed to recognize it.

With the young girl asking what was wrong, she huddled on the floor, holding her knees, rocking and sobbing.

The attendant was bemused. "I also weep occasionally. For myself and for our people. For what the world has become.

"If it's not too much trouble, I would like a lock of your beautiful dark hair, senhora, or perhaps an insignificant tooth, or some other keepsake. We are all heroes."

Steve Simpson lives in Sydney, Australia mostly. He took up writing when the neighbours complained about the bagpipes, and his stories have appeared in various magazines and anthologies. His hobbies include experiments on time travel and negative light, and research on epileptic seizure detection. Web stuff: @inconstantlight inconstantlight.com

Vanity

Kathy Steinemann

Art: Elijah Lin

The vainest ones always die first. The closer they get to death, the more desperate they become.

The average lifespan is now 250 years. Problem is nobody wants to look old. So they come to me. People would rather pay my prices than allow wrinkles and turkey necks to betray their true age.

Many only want a tightening of the jowls. Others a brow lift or a tummy tuck. But some insist on a complete nano rejuvenation. Me? I don't care if I look like a fossil. Or how many kids stare at my old-man wrinkles and white hair. I'll be here long after the narcissists are gone.

I have a successful business—satisfaction guaranteed, reasonable rates. Two credits for a lift or a tuck, one hundred for a nano rejuv. I always warn clients about the potential consequences, but they don't care. The results are worth any price, they say.

I can process a dozen at a time. They lie back, smeared with nanocyte gel and wrapped in expensive spa towels. Then they drift off to sleep in their translucent tubes, listening to soft synth-music in the background, and inhaling sweet scents wafting from the aroma-sims.

Meanwhile, I sit back and smile while my benefits accrue. With every treatment, they shave away their credits, and I reap the rewards.

My machines work—every time. They're miracles, the closest you can come to divinity without being touched by God. With every credit, my machines add a day to my life— and siphon a tenth from theirs.

Like I said, the vainest ones always die first.

Kathy Steinemann, Grandma Birdie to her grandkids, lives in the foothills on the Alberta side of the Canadian Rocky Mountains. She has loved writing for as long as she can remember, and has won multiple public-speaking and writing awards. You can visit her at KathySteinemann.com

---

The Republic of

David

Anton Rose

Art: Monica Burns

I t was **David's time**. A new beginning, on a new world. Sitting on the edge of the bed he ran his fingers up his forearm, feeling the tiny hairs, erect.

The technician entered the room, holding a clipboard. "Good to see you, David," he said. "You look nervous."

David nodded.

"First time?"

"Yes. I've been putting it off for a while."

"There really is nothing to worry about." He handed David the board, which held a contract and a pen.

David scanned the document, only a handful of phrases standing out to him. On the third page, he stopped. "What's this about hallucinations?" he said.

The technician laughed. "Don't worry about that. The technology is perfectly safe these days. That's just for the insurers."

"Will I remember anything about the journey?"

"That's the thing. There is no journey, not really. The machine scans everything and sends the data to your destination. The machine at the receiving end reconstructs you according to the blueprint, molecule for molecule."

David took a deep breath. He signed the paper, and exhaled.

"Have you got anyone there waiting for you?" the technician said.

"My wife and my children went ahead while I finalised some things at this end."

"Well, you'll be seeing them soon."

David opened his eyes. He was lying on a metal slab, naked. He stretched his limbs, feeling the blood push up into his extremities.

Some clothes were waiting for him, folded neatly in a pile. Dressed, he made his way to the door, taking each step deliberately, swaying slightly. He opened the door and saw a mirror, with his reflection in it. But as David stood still, the reflection moved its arm forward, as if to shake his hand. David took a step back. He felt his legs buckle from beneath him, and he collapsed.

When David awoke, he found himself sitting in a soft padded chair. In front of him was another chair, and in it sat a doppelgänger of himself. David lurched forwards, retching.

The other man passed him a glass of water.

"Don't worry about it," he said. "It happens a lot."

David took a sip of the water, and looked at the man. "Who are you?"

"I'm David."

"But I'm David."

"Can't we both be?" The man smiled. There was a knock at the door, and another man entered. He was dressed differently but he, too, was the spitting image of David. He looked at his watch. "Sorry, I'm running a little late."

David stood, and took a few unsteady paces backwards. "What the hell is happening?" he said, saliva sliding off his lips.

The third man approached. "I'm David," he said. "It's nice to meet you."

"This isn't real," said David. "I'm David. Me."

"We don't disagree with you."

David drank the rest of the water. His forehead prickled with sweat.

"Why don't you come and have a seat again?" said the first man. "We can explain everything."

David returned to the chair and passed the glass to the first man. As he took it, David grabbed the man's wrist, squeezing the flesh.

"Don't worry," said the man. "I'm completely real. One hundred percent David."

David sat.

"Do you remember where you were, before this?" one of the men asked.

"I was being transported to one of the new colonies."

"Good. Go on."

"I had a new job out there. My family went ahead while I sorted some things out."

"Perfect."

"But that doesn't explain anything," David said, looking at the two mirror-images sitting in front of him. "It doesn't explain you."

"No, you're right. The machine that brought you here developed a fault. It got stuck in a loop. Six hours after the first David arrived, it created another one. Six hours after that, it did it again. And it never stopped."

"Why don't you turn the machine off?"

"Good question. One, we're not sure that we can. Two, even if we could, we decided against it. We run a democracy of sorts here. One David, one vote."

"This is ridiculous."

"It is a lot to take in."

David stood. He looked at the door. "Where are my family? I want to see them."

The other Davids looked at each other. "You can," they said. "In a way".

They led David out of the building, stepping out into the fresh air.

"I can breathe." David said.

"Yes," said one of the other men. "We've made good progress. The atmosphere is almost Earth-like."

They climbed into the back of a car, which immediately began to move. In the mirror, David saw the face of the driver. It was a reflection of his own face, except that the hair was whiter, the skin more rough.

They sky above glowed with a strange yellow hue, but the streets were filled with familiar sights. All of David's favourite places were there: clusters of pubs with huge screens playing live sports, shops selling clothes and equipment for outdoor activities, and long rows of Mexican restaurants. For the first time since his arrival, David felt hungry.

After a short journey they exited onto a busy street, dotted with tall buildings. There were Davids everywhere, milling around, passing by.

"Where is everyone else?" David asked.

"You mean the other colonists? Some of them stuck around, but most of them left. You can see why, I suppose. This is a world for Davids now."

They entered the tallest building David could see and took the lift to the top floor. The roof of the building had been made into a garden with small trees, bushes, and a cornucopia of luscious flowers; scarlet roses, violet agapanthuses, and bright golden tulips. As they walked down a narrow gravel path, David spotted some small bunches of gypsophila. "They're my wife's favourites," he said.

"We know," the other men said.

At the other side of the roof was a small wall, over which David could see a wide expanse of earth, where the edge of the city melted into dark red hills, and a river snaked into the distance.

Underneath the wall, set into a wide patch of grass, were three gravestones.

"I'm sorry," said one of the men.

"Sorry for what?"

The man gestured towards the gravestones.

As David read the names, he dropped to his knees.

"How?" he said, his voice trembling.

"We're not sure, but we know they all lived long lives."

David turned around. There were tears on his cheeks.

"What do you mean? That's impossible."

"Come on, David," said the first man, his tone sharpening. "There have been many Davids before you, and there will be many Davids after you."

David rose to his feet. As if he was drunk, he staggered over to the wall. "This is bullshit," he said. "I'm still in the machine. I'm going to wake up, and I'll be there, and I'll see them."

"Listen, David," said the other man. "We know it's difficult to accept."

David clambered onto the wall. Looking down he could see hundreds of little Davids, scurrying along the streets. He felt the breeze, pushing against his chest.

"You don't want to do this," the first man said.

David stepped backwards, and fell.

"David!" the first man shouted. "David!" He lifted his hands to his face and rubbed his eyes. "Damn it," he hissed.

The other man took a phone out of his pocket. He dialled a number and held the phone to his head.

"David, hi," he said. "I'm afraid we've had another jumper."

Anton Rose lives in Durham, U.K. He writes fiction and poetry, and would like to be a football player and/or rock star when he grows up. He's 26. Find him at antonrose.com, or @antonjrose

Blasting into the future, across alien worlds and distant galaxies, fantastic technologies and potential threats to humanity,
Where Rockets Burn Through brings science fiction and poetry together in one explosive, genre-busting collection.

Discover an array of poems by more than forty contemporary UK writers, including Edwin Morgan, Jane Yolen, Ron Butlin, WN Herbert, Ken MacLeod and Kirsten Irving, plus an exclusive essay on Sci-fi poetry by Steve Sneyd.

Preface by Alasdair Gray.

£9.99 paperback

Published by *Penned in the Margins*
www.pennedinthemargins.co.uk

LOT 38
FEMALE
19 YEARS
ENGLISH AND SPANISH
SPOKEN
NO KNOWN DEFECTS
FORMER LACROSSE
PLAYER
NO SPECIALIZED
SKILLS

A Season of Want

Ken Poyner

Art: Howard Watts

Only the very rich can afford not to die. Even the moderately rich do not have the resources to be resurrected as cybercitizens. You have to have your financial fingers into everything. Your funds need to make you indispensable—and, consequently, rich enough to have a life assurance contract that puts you into the nanocarbon and metal housing of your choice, when the time of expiration hits you.

George knew that it would take perhaps years for some of the synaptic connections in his brain to meld properly with the adapting electronic leads. Touch was just not the analysis of pressure points and abrasion. The mind had to rewire itself as well, to come up with the sensation of touch all over again, and bond it to a new type of data stream unabashedly coming in. This took will and science and—why not say it?—talent. It is not for the less gifted.

He had not been to an auction since his death. He had not been to much of anything, really. Until very recently, it took all of his time to get the hang of operating robotic arms, flexing plastijoints and deftly manipulating an omnigrasp. It took time to understand that, when he felt tired, he might just be standing in a region of shadow and his battery could be too low to make up for what his solar array was missing. And pressure was hard to learn: push open the door, not punch straight through it. These things take months; but at least he was able to go through the process.

"I think they are going to come out with the cheap ones in a minute."

Beside him, a squat canister of a machine, one of the old, now frowned-on types, extended a stalk eye to look up at the stage, and added to his earlier proposition, "No, it won't be long now."

It took a while to sense speech as speech. At first, it was just a dull thud at the base of what would have been his left big toe, if he were still alive and had toes. But it had come around, and he could now tell this was speech, communication, and not a nail in the foot or a breeze on the back of the neck.

The canister looked over at him. "You know, they always bring out the useless ones first. They slowly ratchet up your expectations. Sometimes I think these first few are not really for sale. They just want to set you up."

George turned his head to eye the speaker with his best-in-class eyes. "It's my first auction in a while. I might have lost the full appreciation of how much gamesmanship goes into it."

The canister returned its stalk eye to its socket. "Well, if you are here, you've done some gamesmanship in your time, too. You can't afford one of these," he thumped himself on the side with a telescoping arm, "if you haven't put

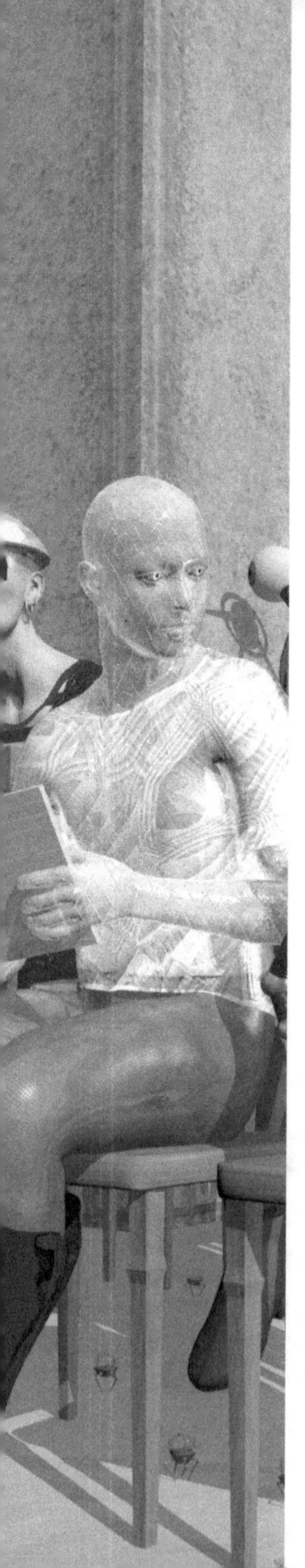

by a few winnings during your life."
It all gets back to what you can afford.
George Fromm, the oxygen salesman, selling
air to entire continents and their gasping
citizens. What can George afford? George
can afford to cheat death. George Fromm,
died the first time on October 13, 2117. Died
again? No, never again.

George glanced across the crowd and saw
that better than two-thirds of them were
cybercitizens. Still, a few reeking, heaving
biological magnates were in attendance, but
their numbers had been dimming for years.
One day, soon, they would be rare in any
place that meaningful business is done.

"Well, since this is my first time in a while,
are there any hints you can give me?" George
said.

"Yes. Don't bid against me."

George was pondering whether he wanted to
continue this conversation, when the first
item came up for bid. It was a man of forty,
according to the public information screen
behind him. The rest of the item's history
flashed below the identifying tag.
Accountant. No known health issues.
Appendix removed.

Nobody bid. What would George need with
an old accountant? He had an ancillary
attachment now that fed the status of his
corporate holdings directly into his forebrain.
Maybe the old canister would need him, or
perhaps one of the still-living bidders would

feel better with a biological unit keeping his numbers clean. Likely, the canister would be better off just ordering an upgrade. The breath-and-sweat crowd? No one made a move to offer even the lowest acceptable bid, and the man was quickly moved off.

The next was a woman close to fifty, with a resume that listed domestic service, and one bad knee. Again, not even the minimum bid. A bad knee on a marginal offering would be enough to kill any deal. George was beginning to think these first items were just a warm up. He had seen the play many times before. Let the bidders get settled, let them get a feel for the auction's geometry, let them scope each other out and see who could be a rival, who might be an ally, who really didn't care about anything but winning.

The crowd had shifted its attention. A biological unit was arguing with a new model cybercitizen. Two cart venders were hawking something at the far back of the crowd. A surveillance drone rattled by.

Everyone surely knew the woman was a teaser, a place holder. She was moved off the far end of the stage, soon to act as filler in a later auction, held elsewhere.

After that came a 2005 Ford Focus. Fairly good condition, with mostly original parts. Just a smattering of synthetics here and there to make it safe to be near. A museum piece, or something to hold a house party around. George thought of bidding, but he had no room for it, and he could not even fit in it. A conversation topic, nothing more. A piece of ancient history he might keep with his hundreds of other pieces of ancient history, which he had collected when artifacts of ancient history had been the rage. When something falls out of favor, you have to warehouse it. A lot of bother.

It wasn't until the seventh or eighth item that a bid was placed: a minimum bid on a length of hand woven Afghan carpet. Not all that useful, but rare ever since Afghanistan was erased. The frill at the carpet's edge could be downright dangerous. The new owner would need to take care when he displayed it. Liability lawsuits can gum up any cozy display of boundless wealth. Properly encased and free from deterioration, the investment might appreciate. Or something even rarer could come onto the market and the investment would stagnate. These sorts of transactions are risky, unless you really want the item. But, in the end, anything someone picks up gets judged by its investment potential. So, even if you want the rare carpet, what you get each day is the data track stating how valuable it is in a volatile market.

George was beginning to wonder why he had come, what his plan had been. The canister was obviously looking for something. Others in the crowd were no doubt waiting for some particular item to come up. Yet others were comparing bargains, looking to play the resale market. George wondered what piece he was looking for. He had been adjusting to his own death, and meticulously sorting out the curiously served inputs that his new cyberbody was feeding him. He wanted more. His desire was always for more— even after death, he still wanted more. He had left the body behind and come into the rebirth of limitless life and everlasting property rights. But he wanted more. More. He just did not know what it was that he wanted more of.

He thought the auction might sort it out, might provide him the stimulus that would match his constitutional insatiability. Each day he was becoming ever more efficient in his afterlife, matching himself to the mechanical, learning to map his old senses and feelings to his new data feeds, inputs and interrupts; but was he becoming ever more

effective, ever more happy, ever more complete in accumulation, ever more true to his self-given purpose?

Thirty-seven items into the auction and he was about to leave, when a girl was brought up in offer. She stood, hands clasped in front of her; her soulless brown hair drifting down over her shoulders and making coy curls at the top of her chest. She kept still, her eyes emptily focused on the front line of the audience: solid. On the screen she was listed as nineteen, no known defects, former lacrosse player, no injuries, bilingual with New English and Spanish, no specialized skills.

George regarded her for a while, and then felt the slightest twinge at the center of his back. Or what his brain thought was his back, as he had had no back ever since his death. But there was this strange, not unpleasant sensation— a paste of ignition on a pool of imaginary, geometric emotions. One reminiscent of what he would occasionally feel in life during those gleeful years when he had mistresses and secretaries who doubled as mistresses and wives. There had been wonders of women in his life, spattered across his days as only they can be spattered for a seriously wealthy man. Since his death, he had no need of the complementary sex. His own sex was just a matter of convenience—he had thought of himself as male in life, so why not continue the idea in death? It does no harm. But it does not matter.

The girl's hands, held in front of her, seemed less submissive than prepared, yet the shoulders dipped down and the head tended deferentially forward. Collateral on a loan, perhaps. Her athleticism stood out, and her lines were serious and tight. She must have a pertinent elasticity. There would be thunderstorms in her; though, over time, she might be a steady rain.

George looked over to the canister, who was watching the crowd and not the stage. No doubt, the canister was looking over the reactions of bidders, looking for stooges, for stand-ins, for people who, probably like himself, were here simply to get a fix on the subsidiary markets: to mix, as only a dead citizen can, the probabilities for resale with the intuition of market vagaries. The canister did not have an interest in this offering; nor, it seemed, did any others in the audience.

A bland biological unit. Born once, like himself, but apparently unable to force herself to achieve anything like he had achieved. Placed in auction for one reason or another—debt, or in exchange for sustenance, or as a serial extension on a family's generational deep oxygenation plan. He held the options on many such plans.

George reached inside himself to see if he could draw out the smoky sensation, if he could taste the edge of its fickle electricity. The feeling was becoming ever more familiar to him with each rattling half-second weathered. There was some sort of drive in this chemical ledge, some matrix of hot and cold pushing across the same landscape, creating. Begetting. There was the sense, yes, of more. More to gather, more to take, more to withhold, more to enslave, more to own, more to enjoy, more to define, more to simply spring into being out of elements collected. He had to roll this itch about, to place it where it should be, or give it a new home where it could grow and feed and maybe devour. More. Yes, more.

The girl looked slowly and willfully across the whole of the audience, her shape imprinting its data pathway on George: bends and folds and stretches and breathing, real breathing. Storms, and a clearing at morning.

George tried to ease the sensation in his long-missing back, to find its connection, to encapsulate it into a unit he could manage, to find a description more useful and less illustrative. He felt the quiver almost like sand in honest, animal fingers. George edged himself sideways, to block the curious stalk eye of the canister. Just before the intriguing girl was led off—to be kept perhaps as a profitless teaser for the next auction's crowd—George reached forward elegantly, holding back the sudden stream of his impossible expectations, and tried to fondle (with an open register) the bizarre and morbidly welcomed sensation that was growing within his adapting circuitry. With perfect pitch and the round O of a chanter's last canticle, for the first time in his afterlife, he pushed his dizzying bid button.

Ken Poyner's fiction and poetry has appeared in such diverse places as *The Alaska Quarterly Review, Poet Lore, Asimov's Science Fiction, Corium, Menacing Hedge, The Legendary, Full of Crow*, and dozens of other print and digital venues. He has been nominated for three Pushcart Prizes, and taught on a National Endowment for the Arts Community Teaching Fellowship. He resides in southeastern Virginia, with his power-lifter wife and various house animals.

The Child with Wings

Ann Craig

Art: Becca McCall

The underground station in the early evening had taken on a strange whispering atmosphere. Perhaps some stray wisp left behind from a thousand rushing souls. Ann had waited till after the rush hour to get home and was now thankful for the quietness this late in her pregnancy. The flickering strip lights exuded a low hum and cast a dull glow over the few folk on the platform. All colours were muted, apart from those on the child. She sat there on the tiled seat, legs dangling, serene in her own small pool of radiance, her wings fluttering in the constant warm breeze from the tunnels.

Her face was pale, making deep pools of her eyes. Her hair was long and tangled, hanging around hunched small shoulders, but her wings were iridescent and seemed to catch every colour of the rainbow. The adult who sat beside her was texting, eyes concentrated on her mobile phone. Ann gazed in fascination at those wings, unable to drag her eyes away and then realised the child was looking directly at her. There was no childishness anywhere in that steady gaze, just a quiet wisdom.

The train arrived in a rush of sound and smells, disturbing the strange inertia that was starting to creep over Ann. She stepped forward and boarded the brightly lit train which had just a scattering of passengers and plenty of seats. The child and the adult appeared in the same carriage and sat across from her slightly to her right.

The train wheezed to a start, seeming to jolt awake the old man who sat in the corner, down from Ann. She watched him raise his head slowly, his eyes immediately finding the child with wings.

Jo

Jo Chambers was eighty two years old today and as he sat wrapped in his tweed coat, dozing, he wondered if there was anyone in the world left who knew that fact. Not that he'd celebrated birthdays for many a long year, not since his Janet had passed, but still, it would be good to think someone still remembered. Then he saw the child sitting on the seat across from him and those wings begged his attention. He stared, loving the look of them as they shone in the artificial fluorescence of the carriage lights. The child stared back at him with huge dark eyes and he fell into memories of other eyes, just as dark and just as beautiful; his Janet. He remembered her wonderful laugh. It was another birthday years ago when the cake she had made for him sank in the middle. She had filled it with custard, and there on that train, he could hear her laugh once again, loud and infectious, at the sight of the lighted birthday candles slowly sinking into depths of the too thin pudding. Jo laughed out loud at the lovely memory of that moment then closed his eyes again, now feeling a deep sense of contentment.

Ross

Ross McLean sat slumped in a heap, his head leaning against the partition glass, eyes down. The coolness of the glass reminding him fleetingly of the morning breeze over the loch. As the child walked passed him to her seat he had noticed her small feet and something bright falling to the ground. He glanced up then to see the wings on her back shiver as she walked, and shift higher as she found her place on the bench. He looked down again to see what she'd dropped.

It lay bright, small and profound. He felt compelled to stretch down to retrieve it. It wasn't easy, it was as though he was pushing against a strong current but he persevered till his hand was almost touching the object. Then the spell was broken by a long leg and an amused voice of another passenger boarding after the child.

"Have you found what you are looking for? Can I get past now?"

Ross looked up to a vivid smiling face with red hair swinging under a bright green beanie hat.

"I'm so sorry, no please its ok" he stammered, his apology trailing off as she laughed.

"Och its fine, ok if I sit here?" Her Scottish accent was like balm on his lonely ears. He stared again at the floor but there was nothing there.

"Are you sure you haven't lost something important? Can I help you find it?" her concern real.

"I think I have" his own voice resonant with the sound of home and his smile matching hers.

Sam

Sam Parish hated undergrounds, hated stations; he pretty well hated everything outside his own home and only left it when there was no choice. He hated strangers getting so close he could feel their breath on his skin, smell what they'd last eaten. Sounds were louder—alien and frightening. He especially despised people who laughed and talked loudly to each other in public. He knew he appeared sullen and unfriendly and he hated it when he found anyone looking at him. He scowled at the young pregnant woman sitting opposite. He condemned his fellow passengers, all on a different planet from him, all able to read the incomprehensible writing on the maps and adverts that festooned the train. As the new passengers boarded, he kept his feet stuck out, took up more than a seat's worth of room on the benches, everything saying *keep off*. Then when the child had appeared, she had climbed up to sit right beside him.

Her wings had touched his hand as she squirmed her small body up on to the seat. His hand burned as though he had held ice too long, his whole body shivered. There she was, her eyes turned up to his, so plainly asking for help, so very scared, he never wondered why the adult with her was not helping.

"I don't like underground trains either, don't be scared, it's just a strange noise and smell, but it's OK" his voice gentle and reassuring, very unlike his usual growl. Her eyes were liquid and shining and he thought tears might fall.

"I can't read you know, but those map things up there, they tell you when it's your stop. I have to count because someone told me how many stations I had to go, you could ask someone how many you had to go and you could count."

She looked at him and her little face lit up with such a grateful smile that it felt as though strong sunlight had fallen on him. The warmth from it soaked into him, melting away the icebergs which always lurked beneath his skin, ready to do damage. He stood up, smiling down at her, again the wings brushed his hand and this time it felt like a warm caress. He straightened his back and with unusual grace and ease, he left the train at the next stop..

Ann

Ann moved her feet out of the way of the man as he left, amazed at the quiet smile on his transformed face, and then once more she studied those wings. They were perfect, dainty and shimmering. She looked at the child sitting with her small legs sticking out from the too large bench, her tiny hands balancing her, splayed out at either side. She had a look of determination on her small unremarkable face.

Ann saw the wings just peeping above her shoulders, rising and falling as the child breathed in and out. The movement was hypnotic and she felt her own breath slow to match the rhythm of the wings. She could feel her breath merge with the child's until they were breathing as one. The world slipped away, till all that was left was the rhythm of that breath, in and out, and the deep beat of that heart. As the train slowed to a stop, Ann blinked and with a grave reluctance let go of that other heartbeat. The lights were harsh and flickering, the noise an unpleasant persistent presence.

The child had never looked her way again and she never spoke to the adult with her, not a word. The next stop would be Ann's. She stood up, ungainly, holding the rail to keep steady, reluctant to take her eyes from the child. Then everything lurched sideways. At first she thought it was the train but then she felt the wet between her legs and pain pull at her back. She sat back down confused and shocked, too early she thought, not here, not now. They had said this was her last chance and she had never managed to carry a pregnancy this long. Then she stopped thinking as more pain swept over her and she heard herself make a noise and then nothing.

When she opened her eyes she was lying on the floor, the vibration of the moving train almost a comfort. She was wrapped in a warm tweed coat. There was the young boy cradling her head, a girl with red hair held her hand and an old man kneeled on creaking knees beside her. They told her not to worry, it would all be fine, and an ambulance was waiting for her at the next station. Ann was not worried, she felt strangely calm, all seemed quiet and still to her as if the world was holding its breath, sounds muffled by the circle of these concerned strangers.

Ann looked around not quite remembering what she was searching for, but there she was smiling down at her, the wings now the merest suggestion of light, the vision of her fading already.

Ann whispered, "will you please stay this time?"

The child smiled with love and nodded, her features blurring till she was no more.

Ann sighed and started to push, and the memory of those exquisite wings gently floated away.

Ann Craig hails from Glasgow but has lived in a village perched on cliffs on the north east coast of Scotland for the last 40 years. The first book she remembers reading was *Dune*. Her only disappointment in her various career paths was they never did take her into space. She lives in hope. Ann likes philosophy, community, family, friends and fantasy: preferably all mixed in together.

SF Caledonia

Duncan Lunan *has many strings to his bow, as a researcher, tutor, critic, editor, lecturer and broadcaster—chiefly on astronomy, spaceflight and related subjects. Best known today as a non-fiction author, his books include* Man and the Stars *(1974),* Man and the Planets *(1984) and* Incoming Asteroid! *(2013). Yet his influence on science fiction writing, especially in Scotland, has been significant—in part due to his role in the launch of the Glasgow Science Fiction Writers Circle, 'alumni' of which include Gary Gibson, Michael Cobley and Hal Duncan. He also edited* Starfield: Science Fiction by Scottish Writers, *the first anthology of its kind, published in 1989.*

*-**Paul F Cockburn***

Paul F Cockburn talks to Duncan about his writing life, but first we have a previously unpublished story. *Last Days in the Nanotech War* was accepted by John F. Carr and Jerry Pournelle for their *There Will Be War* series, but the series was terminated before it appeared.

Last Days in the Nanotech War

Duncan Lunan

Art: Michael Dabrowski

1. A hot bath will do you good

Kennedy was on a last scouting of the outskirts of this latest village, late in the afternoon, when one of the Gurkhas stepped from behind a whitewashed wall and beckoned him across. His first reaction was to slip off the safety catch on his assault rifle, thinking they had found a nest of sleeping vampires, but the Nepalese soldier waved that away. He was to follow, and keep quiet, with a last look over the fields.

It seemed obscenely wrong for the weather to be so good. After the Bomb was supposed to be dark, cold, perpetual rain, not this wonderful summer with unharvested fields of corn rippling in the heat-haze: van Gogh with fallout. The retreat to Dunkirk might have been like this, though there was no Luftwaffe overhead this time. Probably there were no flightworthy aircraft in the world by now, though there could be vampires out there with laser sights and recycled stealth electronics. And the numbers in retreat were fewer this time: just the British garrison from Gibraltar, and some units which had been with the UN further along the Mediterranean, trying to get back to the home country across France. They had made it a long way, too, out of Spain and up to Le Mans, before what used to be motor racing fans had immobilised the last of their vehicles.

The last message from the English High Command had specified a rendezvous in "the temporary island of Wales". Their own country had been host to nuclear weapons for so long that they couldn't be surprised by what had happened; though as the Aussies said, being Poms no doubt they'd whinge regardless, any that were left. As a New Zealander, Kennedy partly agreed, though with less cynicism. What was to happen in Wales—or on Wales, you had to say now—nobody seemed to know. Some final cataclysmic battle? Reactivate a ground terminal and send the vampires' control units a terminal command? Some of the men at least seemed to believe they would awaken Merlin, like in that last fantasy best-seller before the war. He could swear many of them thought they were living it.

The sunshine meant that even on foot, the units could leave the previous night's attackers behind, sleeping in hedgerows and woods where cover could be found. But after dark they would catch up, flowing silently around whatever wrecked village had become the latest bivouac—they had the night vision to do it. The local vampires knew they were coming and would wait, so each night, now, the attackers were in greater numbers when they came. The soldiers snatched sleep as early in the night as they could, knowing what would come later. But no-one had slept soundly for weeks.

The Gurkhas' sergeant was waiting with two more of his men, in the roofless bathroom of the ruined villa. Sunlight reflected from a tiled wall and a broken, full-length mirror, but was creeping up from the littered floor as the sun went down. At their feet was a sunken bath, filled with sinister-looking, bright red liquid. But it couldn't be blood, which would already be starting to congeal. It had come from the tins the sergeant showed him, marked with the magic word, 'Accelerator'—the artificial enzymes the two sergeants had been seeking since their escape together from sick-bay the day it all went wrong. This was the only way of triggering the bugs' end-cycle if you didn't rate an implanted control unit, as of course Other Ranks didn't... though that had saved Kennedy and the Gurkha from a much worse fate.

"I found the tins in an outhouse, Kennedy sahib, and I filled the bath with rainwater myself. The seals on the tins were unbroken, and the sun has heated the bath throughout the day. I have tried the healing power myself, and it is effective." Indeed, as his eyes adjusted from the glare outside, he could see the red sheen on the older man's skin, brighter than the natural pigment. With nightfall it wouldn't be noticeable, even in firelight.

"Send for one of the medics, then."

"There is no time for that, sahib. The sun will soon be down." The solar heat was the only chance, with no electrical power available. If the enzymes weren't above their activation temperature, then instead of turning off the bugs in his bloodstream after absorption through his skin, they would nourish increased activity. By nightfall this bath would be a stimulant for their enemies.

Was it worth the risk? Anything to stop the little bastards mining his bloodstream, endlessly rebuilding the knee-brace he no longer needed. Anything to get off a diet secretly dominated by iron and magnesium tablets which were ever harder to find. He could strip off before these men as he couldn't before his own, because of the secret they shared. The British troops had reached a stage where they were becoming irrationally afraid of all technology, let alone the nanos, and the three equally spaced short cylinders of gleaming steel protruding yet again above his knee were all too plain a giveaway; whereas the loyalty of the Gurkhas to their Non-Coms had let them live with their sergeant's equivalent. The three stubs were nearly long enough to grip with the bolt-cutters again: each with its perfect little screw and washer which excruciatingly were formed before the cylinder was extruded through his flesh. Only pain-killers made the march possible for him: only the medics knew it. If he let them grow much further the stubs would turn downwards, blindly programmed to immobilise the joint.

At first he lowered only the affected limb into the fluid, but the effect was so good that he levered himself fully into the bath, immersing himself twice. The sweat and the aches of the day's march seemed to float away: would the stubs do the same, as the enzymes reached and turned off the fiendish little machines? He sat up, peering through the scarlet liquid at the knee, and experimentally wiggled the first of them. It broke away, leaving a thin stream of real blood, but there was clean scar tissue in the indentation it left behind, not the open wound he'd expected. The other two cylinders came the same way, for good, all being well, and he was as near as possible to fully healed when he arose.

It seemed criminal to pull the plug, letting the precious fluid drain away, when it might be such succour to the infected wounded before they moved on. But with sunset the vampires would be stirring—first the local ones, already out there, later the accumulated force from last night and all the other nights, catching up with the column under the Moon. This far out of the village, the house was undefendable in darkness: the bath would have given aid and comfort to the enemy, and been fatally contaminated by morning.

2. You wonder how it all came about

The hospital doctors, of course, had been in the best position to know what was happening, even as they found themselves compelled to destroy their equipment and attack their patients in nightmare reversal of the Hippocratic Oath. Moving from floor to floor, hiding in cupboards and stairwells, the two sergeants had overheard enough during their escape for Kennedy to understand the downfall of civilisation. It was possible that he was among the best-informed, yet uninfected, in what was left of the world.

He had had to sign an agreement not to have nanotech implants while he remained a Regular. Healing bugs might be useful but you had to have an implanted programme unit to control them, and that was too vulnerable to ElectroMagnetic Pulse or other enemy interference. Look at what had happened to all those civvy users now... and you couldn't have squaddies on parade with all kinds of cosmetic fads and exotic hardware growing on them, any more than a 2000s sergeant would have allowed the troops to drill wearing Walkmans, or an earlier one would have tolerated punk hairstyles. It was different for Reservists, who couldn't be expected to forego the benefits of the nanotech revolution in everyday life. They had been expected to avoid the more flamboyant options voluntarily, but the poor bastards couldn't help themselves now.

It was all so simple, at first: once the bugs in your bloodstream insured your health and fitness, what about modifications? Page through the catalogue, see what cyborg implants you would like;

the control unit would programme the bugs, you took the dietary supplements; they built the receptors, you plugged in the devices. In theory the bugs would build into you anything you wanted, from a permanent Walkman to a full-fledged Virtual Reality unit, night sight, telescopic vision, as long as you had the control box to programme them, the appropriate designer chips, and some way of ingesting the raw materials. In reality the reprogrammed bugs were lazy: they'd rebuild minimal bone and nerve connections to spec and then list for you the components to order and plug in.

It didn't end there, of course. Consumerism had to speed up the process. How much easier to have a catalogue chip, updated each time you used your built-in mobile satellite link to access the latest book, video or music! You could make your selection anywhere, anytime, and it was all so cheap and easy—but not yet cheap and easy enough.

Biowar experts had supposed a tailored virus could bring down civilisation, but it took their analog, a computer virus, to do it. It wasn't even clear that it had been economic warfare and not just an excessive desire to boost catalogue sales. All it took was one modification: not only could you make a choice at any time but you had to make a choice, the catalogue chip and the medic programme would flip endlessly through the options till you picked one, in your sleep if necessary. The reprogrammed bugs fed you back a demand for raw materials and already existing components which couldn't be satisfied by mail. The afflicted couldn't wait to order the goods, much less budget for them—it had to be now, even if it meant literally tearing civilisation apart, even if governments first threatened and then used nuclear weapons to stop the plague from spreading. The sensation was said to be like the 'phantom limb' of an amputee, except that this was a compulsion to build something on. It translated into a hunger to raid storehouses, strip down machines, looking for the right resistors, printed circuits, lenses, whatever might be needed to fill the 'missing' list. Suddenly everyone was a mechanic, trying to placate their inner demons with the wail 'I'm sorry, I couldn't get the parts'. Turning off the satellites was far, far too late.

Computer stores were looted overnight. The electronic hobbyists' bins of scrap components became a deadly lure to vampires, promising a banquet but always triggering new torture as your system recognised part of some other device and began, with or without your conscious will, to modify you to incorporate it. In every house in every town Kennedy had found appliances pulled apart, chassis and wiring harnesses thrown into corners after anything usable had been cannibalised. In every home office or den there were eviscerated computers, smashed screens, gutted keyboards and backless printers. Cars stripped by a new and more desperate type of thief lined every town and village street.

In the military it was worst for the Commandos and other Special Forces, who had been fitted with programmers and whose catalogues were of military hardware. Having stripped the stores of military bases they now haunted the recent battlefields, building themselves into ever more elaborate Walking Weaponry. Fortunately nonspecific troops like Kennedy's had little of the really high-tech gear to attract them, and had managed to get out of Gibraltar while the first battles raged around them. Sooner or later each affected unit would build in a siren and set it off, luring others to a battle for components, in which one or both contestants would at last find peace.

For most people suicide was harder, with your blood seething with repair units to close and heal even major wounds, and metabolise the effect of poisons. They could even 'rebuild' a head shot, rebuild the biological brain. Of course the rebuilt segments would be blank. Kennedy had only survived the bugs he'd had, the ones the bath had deactivated, because his knee injury was before the disaster and hadn't rated implanting a control unit. The bugs were mono-programmed and the virus couldn't reach them to trigger new demands. But if you didn't have a controller and were infected with a reprogrammed variety of bug, you were in living hell—adapted to plug in some device, compelled to do so (one component at a time if need be), but with no idea what it was you had to have. And you had to have food sources for the bugs, and blood, with its high iron content, was the obvious choice.

The vampires had many weapons, since they could design and create their own. A favourite was a needle extruded from the wrist —even when deployed it could be hidden until too late, the stabbing deadly handshake. Mixing of body fluids was always the aim—in exchange for the blood extracted you got Super-AIDS to knock out the immune system, nanotech cells to replace it, leaving you dependent on them forever. But if there weren't enough bacterial cells to attack, not enough food for the latest reconstruction, they turned on the body's own cells, especially red corpuscles—hence the anaemic pallor and the avoidance of sunlight. An intravenous infusion of someone else's blood—the more different group the better, but that wasn't much help in a regiment with a family structure like this one—gave the hungry bugs new targets and let the host body rally for a time.

The enemy didn't like mirrors, and neither would you, thought Kennedy, if you looked like that. Garlic was no damned use, though, nor crosses. They might have built-in radar, but at least they couldn't turn themselves into bloody bats. They hadn't resorted to nukes once they possessed them—a waste of potential food and parts. Chemical warfare stocks were all long since destroyed. If any archives of tailored viruses survived—true biochemical ones—only the vampires could use and could release them with impunity. To them, they were just more food for the bugs, but for humanity, it would be the final end.

Part of the nightmare was that the standard control package always seemed to include the same entertainments chip, the same best-seller from just before the war, so that every victim spoke in the same fantasy dialogue. The book had been so intensively hyped, probably everyone who had access to a terminal had read it or been treated to excerpts. Kennedy had read it in sick-bay. It could even have been the vehicle for the computer virus—it

wouldn't have affected him without a control unit. The book, its imagery, its music had been everywhere. It was unbearable in a voice you knew:

"Michael, Michael, you can't know what this is like. Share with me, my brother, ease my pain for a while, and after we shall hunt together with a stronger bond than blood between us..."

Send out a burst of fire, be it bullets or be it napalm, anything to stop that whining appeal. He'd have wanted it in his true self if he could have asked for it. Did I get him? Would Mum and Dad have understood?

When the vampires came out of the cornfields, they overran the town regardless of casualties. They weren't going to shoot at themselves by accident, or their prey; there might come a time when they attacked one another for components, but so far the fraternity of their radio links prevented that. Attacking through the roof was easy for them with built-in power tools or hardened steel fingernails. The man across the street was covering that for you, but was vulnerable himself to a ground-level rush, especially from the rear. Shooting them was risky because body fluids could splash, get into your eyes, mouth or open wounds; flame-throwers were better but obviously risky at close quarters.

Once there were fires going, however, their light helped. It was street corner and house-to-house fighting, but without the stones, petrol bombs and Kalashnikov sniping; in this the enemy were always going hand-to-hand if they could. Crouching at the entry to a firelit square, blasting at a shadowy form on a rooftop, realising from the chaos inside the house that he hadn't got them all in time... indoors himself, giving first-aid, warned by the cracking of the plaster above, shooting upwards at a pale apparition revealed as his gunfire stripped the ceiling to the joists. Somewhere a voice kept screaming *No! No! No!* in the lulls of the battle. Not clear whether resisting attack or the pangs of a new hunger after inoculation. Nobody was going that way to find out.

And it went on like that, hour after hour, as on so many other nights—a recurring nightmare of collapsing ceilings, burning stairwells, soldiers dragged down in gardens and alleys, always just where you hadn't covered in time, too late to get to... you had to cover your own back. Get a grenade on the launcher if you could, fire it where you last saw movement, hope with luck you got victim and attacker both. If you came upon a body, hit it with the flamethrower to be certain, and the same for a buddy, preceded by a high-velocity round, if he asked for it... If you caught them feeding, let all the group have it with whatever weapon came first to hand.

Eventually, dawn would come. The one consolation was that in Europe, in summer, the nights were short. In his native New Zealand the army would have had no chance, probably all gone in the first long night.

3. Many were undead by the morning

His last redoubt had been a single-story cottage, stone-walled, with an attic floor above too solid to shift without giving warning, and the rear collapsed into impenetrable rubble. There he waited it out as the scene outside grew paler and the shooting died away. Outside in a pile of ash was the skeleton of a little girl, burned almost to powder, irretrievably mixed up with the remains of her powered, computer-controlled wheelchair. He felt no compunction about having ended her (as no doubt she would have him) because she was already on fire when she rolled down the street to pass him. At the second flamethrower hit, the mag-alloy wheels had burned like flares and now only the ceramic superconductor coils were left, disintegrating at a touch.

The first priority was the roll-call; then the body-count. The reason for stopping in small villages was so that the bodies could be found and tallied quickly. Then the list of 'missing in action'; finally, the repeated roll-call of the living, to be written down, circulated, memorised. At any checkpoint, tonight, these and only these were the friends you would allow to 'advance and be recognised.' Anyone else, however familiar, however plausible, would be cut down at once: *They took me prisoner, mates, but I got away from them* was a line that nobody on guard in the dusk would fall for again.

Their secure store had been breached, ransacked by vampires and then by other units moving out ahead of them. The worst offenders there had been led by their own senior officer's brother, and among the men there were mutterings about whether he might not have been infected. Backpacks and carrying cases of all kinds were a premium, now they'd lost their transport, and after the plundering a lot of the stuff that was left would have to be abandoned. Sorting through the shambles Kennedy found a pair of binoculars, without the case, and put them round his neck because nobody else seemed to want them. The unit was being disabled by fear of mechanical things and of what they might be assembled into, taking it out on their own 'electronics wizard.'

The soldiers were being taken over by that fantasy, he was convinced—starting to talk the way the vampires did, to use battle-cries from the book, to act out the prejudices of its spear-carriers. Young Jimmy, their last technician, whom everyone had once admired, was coming in for a lot of stick even as he did wonders matching up bits, making partial reassemblies, not even knowing yet if anything could be put back together to work. Despite his importance to them, for days now he had been saddled with the dirty jobs by the men, and even as he worked he was assailed by stupid questions from the officers. "No, sir, we don't have enough for individual backpacks any more, we have to pool what's left. Yes, sir, even clothing and towels."

"What about water, sir?" one of the men helpfully put in. "What we have left is barely fit for washing, let alone drinking."

The first officer ignored it, but there was always another. "Washing water d'you call this? Good God!"

"I'll get some, sir," said Jimmy. "I heard a tap running across the way." Nobody else moved: reassembling radios was less important. Kennedy had noticed it too, the familiar sound in urban conflict of a broken main—but, he suddenly realised, there had been no piped water here for many weeks. That tap had Dolby sound!

Snatching up his assault rifle, Kennedy plunged out into the street, only to be slowed as the damned binoculars swung and slammed against his chest. Before he reached the house the tap noise cut off, and he heard Jimmy's scream as a vampire sprang on him from the rafters. As Kennedy crashed into the ruined house the two were already locked in a deadly embrace, needles doubtless fully home—nothing to do but switch to automatic fire and blow both of them away, pasting them into the dissolving wall behind.

Well, he thought, we've lost our wizard. It's getting more like a computer game all the time. The men would be glad of it: they could leave more equipment behind, less for the vampires to come after. It wouldn't help because in this war, equipment at least as good as your enemies' was your only hope. But when I go, he thought, will I be the last to know what was really happening, the rest all caught up in the fantasy appearance?

As the survivors prepared to move out the horseman and woman were there as always, up at the head of the column with the officers—'St. George and his lady'—as the troops had nicknamed them, though they were dressed in leather, not armour. Each morning Kennedy wondered who they were, whether they would ever step out of character from that damned book. His curiosity never drove him to find out and that made him suspect they might not be real. Could there have been a special version of the saga, tailored for the armed forces—some hypnotic construct, backed up perhaps by a special memory-affecting bug? 'Guaranteed to generate a romantic image of leadership if triggered by the stress of warfare'. It had happened spontaneously at Mons, after all, less than a century before, with the hapless troops swearing they went over the top led by an armoured crusader. If these figures were real, they kept resolutely to Officer Country and never seemed to be around for the fighting, yet the men worshipped them without question. He wondered, chillingly, if the Gurkha sergeant had been able to see them, for he took no interest in the book. It was too late now to ask him, lost like so many others in last night's conflict.

As they began to march, the woman's voice floated back to him in song, 'unnaturally clear, methinks' if it was real and without amplification, when she was facing away from him at that distance.

What is this clarion call on the wind as to battle we ride?

Why this effluvium of burned flesh from each haunted village we pass?

The words were remarkably prophetic. Taken from the book, the song was a hit just before the war, back when machines could be trusted, before they had the power to create for you any sort of a world which they thought you wanted.

Interview: Duncan Lunan

by Paul F Cockburn

So, Duncan, when did you realise you would be a writer?

Duncan Lunan: I can remember not being able to read, shortly before my third birthday, and it just came as a package—suddenly I *could* read and I could read anything. I can remember—it might have been as much as a year later—my mother trying to teach me to read from *Rupert Bear* in the *Daily Express*, and I was pretending that I couldn't, and I was meanwhile reading the editorial next to it. I was writing by the time I was four; I even produced a hand-written newspaper. By the time I went to school I had actually started writing poetry, which very quickly got knocked out of me! As the the youngest child in the class, who could already read and write, I was madly popular with an entire class of older children who couldn't. But there it was; I just *was* going to be a writer.

Were you drawn to science fiction at an early age?

DL: Not especially. As regards astronomy and space, I knew it was there. I remember my father stopping the car between Troon and Prestwick to watch the Northern Lights, and they got me up to watch an eclipse of the Moon. That same year, 1950, there was the Blue Sun. That was caused by a smog of oil droplets that had drifted across Greenland and Iceland and back down over Northern Europe from forest fires in Canada. Granny took me down to the beach to see it. And it was totally bizarre; the sun was blue, the sky was bronze, and the whole familiar landscape of Troon beach was alien, and I remember thinking to myself: "This is like being on another planet." I had the concept already by then, being on other planets. But my first love was still the sea.

What converted me was *The Lost Planet* on BBC Radio Children's Hour. And then I started to get into *Dan Dare*; fortuitously (newspaper strip) *Jeff Hawke* started in the *Daily Express* about that time. I bullied my parents into getting the *Young Traveller in Space* by Arthur C. Clarke for my eighth birthday. From then on I was totally hooked by the spaceflight side. I got into *Journey Into Space* with the second serial, but I didn't read a lot beside the comics until a lot later. I got into Arthur C Clarke and Fred Hoyle in my early teens; ironically, it was when I started going to the Scottish branch of the British Interplanetary Society in 1962, that a friend called Andy Nimmo encouraged me to start reading Asimov, Heinlein, Sheckley and Van Vogt – and the whole thing broadened out from there. By the time I got to university, I was reading SF quite avidly.

Troon, a small seaside town in south west Scotland, doesn't strike me as being an easy place to track down science fiction, especially back in the 1950s.

DL: There was a very good bookshop on Ayr Street, Troon, that did have a pretty good selection of SF when I wasn't reading it, but there's an article to be written about the difficulty of getting SF in the 1960s. The magazines *Fantastic* and *Amazing* could only be had from Glasgow's Central and St Enoch Stations; one took one, and one took the other. Even more weirdly, the *Galaxy* group [of magazines]— *Galaxy*, *If*, and *Worlds of Tomorrow* – could only be had from a small chain of three pornographic bookshops surrounding the city's then three railway stations, and they took one each—so you had to visit all three!

The other major channel was to find out where the second-hand bookshops were near the bus stations, because this was where American

"I was writing by the time I was four"

servicemen coming in from the Holy Loch would disembark, and dump a load of paperbacks and magazines to get drink money. There was a very good one on Argyle Street; I had a pretty good working relationship with the chap who ran that. He knew I would be in once a week or so.

So when did you start writing SF?

DL: Again, that was very early on. Once I'd got hooked on *Journey Into Space*, I started writing my own, but I was aware of the inadequacies of most of it. When I was about 13, I wrote one which other people typed up for me, and I sent to Collins and various other people, and received polite replies – "lots of remarkable ideas here, keep at it"—that kind of thing.

Do you remember your first published story?

DL: During the vacations while I was at university, I was writing a novel, and a strange chain of events put me in a position to offer it to John W. Campbell [the writer and editor who arguably shaped the Golden Age of Science Fiction in America—*Editor*]. It all had to do with how we met at the 1965 World Science Fiction Convention in London. I'd come off a Vespa scooter and had cut my knee badly, so I was wearing my father's kilt with the officer's jacket. Campbell wanted to know where he could get a jacket like that. It was one of these quite bizarre moments in one's life, when Mrs John W Campbell said to me: "If you can spare a moment, my husband would like to speak with you." I also ended up escorting his daughter to the banquet. I had no problem with that; she was very nice. The upshot was, trading on that, I was able to write to Campbell and say: "Here is the novel I told you about."

Although he didn't buy it, he got me a contract with the Scott Meredith Literary Agency, which was then the one that all the big SF people were with. Meredith made my first actual sale, which was to *Fantastic* and *Amazing*, in 1967, but that didn't come out until 1974. My first professionally published story was *The Moon of Thin Reality* in *Galaxy* in July 1970; basically a 'spaceship in trouble' story, set inside a Dyson sphere. The editors at *Galaxy* were fooled by it into thinking that I must be an astrodynamist of note, and they wanted to do a profile of me, but dropped the idea when they discovered I wasn't. But they still got their art editor Jack Gaughan to do the cover, and everybody went: "Who is this client of Meredith who gets a Gaughan cover on his first published story?"

> "Who is this client of Meredith who gets a Gaughan cover on his first published story?"

This was enough to persuade my father that I should dump my dead end office job and go full time, which took a little bit of persuasion because my friend Chris Boyce had tried it before me and not made it. He'd had to go back to the newspapers after six months. My father was also wary of the whole deal, but eventually suggested that if I was ever going to be a professional writer, this was the time to do it—so I did, and here I am!

Initially it worked; I started dashing off stories and immediately sold the first three, but I was then cut off from the US market by the 1971 UK postal strike. There was no market on this side of the Atlantic at that time; in any case, my contract with Meredith was exclusive. As I anticipated, when the strike ended there was a glut of stories by British authors competing for slots that had already been filled by US authors during the hiatus. Eventually Meredith did sell four of my stories but what I had realised was: this wasn't going to work, so I started, for the first time since my teens, to write non-fiction again. That led to *Man and the Stars*. Non-fiction has dominated ever since. In that first phase I sold nine stories; I'm now up to 34, but that's after a further 40 years, so it's only very occasionally now that I write fiction. I keep saying I'll go back to it, but there's always another non-fiction opportunity to take up.

Did you ever consider writing a novel?
DL: In fact, I had two big ideas for novel sequences, neither of which got published. I had this big series about a space-line with more than a little influence from my old interest in

the sea; there were definitely echoes of Percy F. Westerman there. But I'm not always at the right place at the right time, even though it was the novel that had convinced John W. Campbell to get me the contract with Meredith. Part of the other idea got ripped off for a television series which, on legal advice, I can't say too much about. I had actually reached the stage of exchanging contracts with Gold Medal Books, who then decided not to do it after all.

The annoying thing is that Meredith later came back to me and said: "The market has opened up for series, and we know you have two unpublished series, do you want to blow the dust off them?" I looked at it, but there simply wasn't time—I was on a deadline with *Man and the Stars* and couldn't do it. So at the point when *Dune* opened up that market, I wasn't in a place where I could take that opportunity. So to this day, no novels; I've got one in mind – well, Mars is in fashion at the moment, and it's a Mars novel. If I ever get all my other commitments out of the way…

You still kept in touch with SF, however, as a reviewer for the then *Glasgow Herald* (now *The Herald*) newspaper.

DL: My achievement, I suppose, was that I got SF to the point that it was being reviewed monthly, where previously it had not been reviewed at all. Then the book editor was replaced by John Linklater, who hated genre fiction and very quickly got rid of me.

With the 200th anniversary of the paper coming up the following year, however, my friend Chris Boyce—by then working there—persuaded them that they should have an SF short story competition. It was extremely successful—the first one attracted over 300 entries, although a full third ended on the line: "And his name was Adam, and her name was Eve."

Then Ann Karkalas, of the Adult & Continuing Education Department at the University of Glasgow, asked if I would do a writing class. So, before returning all the competition manuscripts, I turned the cover sheets of contact details over to the University who did a mail shot to everyone within 50 miles. That ensured enough students for the class to go ahead. Initially it was for 10 weeks, at the end of which—because it had kept up the numbers—Ann asked if they would like a second term. One of the things I'd done towards the end of the first was to run a workshop, and people—Michael Cobley and the rest—said yes, we would like a second term, but we want it to be workshop-based. So the second term was almost entirely workshops and,

at the end of that, basically we all said that we didn't want to stop! So the workshops continued, and have continued to this day.

How important do you think the Circle has been in supporting new authors?

DL: The Circle held a 21st party, during which a toast to me was raised. What I said in reply was: "You'd all have made it under your own individual talents; the most we can say here is that we haven't done you any harm. Hopefully, we've encouraged you and pointed you in the right direction."

What I think I can say is that everybody who has stuck with the Glasgow group has achieved publication of one form or another. But the Circle wasn't my idea. Even having that second term consist of workshops came from the people there. I was just in the right place at the right time to make it happen, and am very pleased about that.

How has SF publishing changed during your lifetime?

DL: Just fairly recently I reviewed Algis Budrys' collected reviews from *Fantasy and*

Science Fiction, for *Interzone*. One of the things he was really concerned about (in the 1970s) was that fantasy looked set to drive SF out of the market altogether. Well that didn't happen; thanks to *Star Wars*, suddenly there was a boom for SF again, but it was action-adventure rather than what tended to be described as more cerebral SF.

What I've become aware of, since I started reviewing for *Interzone* is that there's now a whole new genre of very long, cerebral SF by the likes of Peter Hamilton, which I hadn't really been aware of and am catching up with now.

Also, there are the series which are targeted at a comparatively younger audience, and I don't think they're all that good. With some series, all the good ideas are in the first book. That seem to me the way that things are going, looking at the lists, but there's still good stuff out there.

Is there still a market for short stories?

DL: Well, I certainly hope so! Indeed I think it's an excellent thing that *Shoreline of* *Infinity* has got launched, because there have been at least three attempts since the 1950s to have a science fiction magazine based in Scotland, *Nebula* being the first. It's good to see these guys getting on with it.

Perhaps this is where the influence of electronic publishing impacts; for me it's completely changed things. Print-on-demand technology has made it possible to get back into publishing my kind of book for the first time in years— immediately, four of them! There's a backlog to clear, with at least another four in prospect. But beyond that, I've got other ideas. I've been promising for a couple of years to do a popular version of *Children of the Sky*; now that I've got all the facts out there, I can do the story as a narrative. And there's still that Mars novel. One way or another, I've got all the work I can handle!

Photos of Duncan Lunan: Thomas Brash

Border Crossings

Steve Green

The New Resurrectionists

Even those readers who don't share this magazine's EH postcode will no doubt be aware that the cobbled streets of 1820s Edinburgh were prey to vile predators eager to harvest the weak and vulnerable in order to satisfy a growing industry in medical research. Stumble drunkenly out from a meeting of the city's resident scientific romance society and you'd stand a better than average chance of ending up on an anatomist's slab, being carved up in front of bored medical students wondering why no one had yet invented Rag Week and the Edinburgh Fringe.

However, my focus today is not upon these corrupt and shadowy figures, rather a new breed of vulture dedicated not to the pursuit of corpse-capitalism, but the theft and monetarisation of genuine creators' visions.

The Twisted Shape of Things To Come

I won't bother naming the imprint responsible, since it works on the fringes of real publishing, but I read with some bemusement its August 2014 announcement of plans to "celebrate" the imminent shift of H. G. Wells' science fiction novel *The Shape of Things to Come* out of UK copyright by launching a series of anthologies vampirically leeching off his canon.

I wasn't exactly surprised—the line's editor-in-chief has a track record of disinterring the works of Edinburgh-born author Arthur Conan Doyle and sewing on additional (not to mention unnecessary) text to produce 'steampunk mash-ups'—but I somehow doubted old Herbert would have felt all that celebrated, assuming he hadn't already been deceased for just short of seven decades.

Now, I don't want to leave the impression I'm against all forms of artistic cover version. Kim Newman's 1992 multiple award-winning novel *Anno Dracula*, for instance, is an intelligent and intriguing spin upon Bram Stoker's genre milestone (itself, to be fair, a cocktail of European history and ancient superstitions, not a bad achievement for a theatre manager who never left the British shoreline, let alone that of Infinity). The difference is, Kim produces works such as this and his Superman riff *Ubermensch!* (published a year previously, in the anthology New Worlds 1) because he perceives a kink in the existing track, rather than a siding into which to divert the literary locomotive and strip it for spares.

(Nor am I entirely innocent in this form of enterprise, although my own ambitions extend only as far as publishing an annotated edition of E. M. Forster's astonishingly prescient 1909 short story *The Machine Stops*. Unfortunately, Forster had the temerity to survive until 1970, which means I wouldn't be able to rip off his estate for another quarter-century, even were I to share the same moral blindness as certain others.)

Groundhog Day

Of course, it's not just a deficit in imagination which drives such lazy regurgitation of old ideas: audiences increasingly demonstrate a desire to avoid the unfamiliar, preferring brand name franchises to anything with a spark of actual originality.

Sam Raimi had barely completed work on the third Spider-Man movie when Columbia began planning the reboot, ensuring Andrew Garfield was able to step into Tobey Maguire's boots just five years later, and the process is accelerating: Marvel launches Tom Holland into the role in next year's *Captain America: Civil War*, with a full reboot in 2017, the second in just fifteen years. Only the Tardis has a faster turnstile.

Yes, the Future Has Been Sold

In a recent Daily Telegraph interview, the Oscar-winning film director Robert Zemeckis despaired at the current state of his industry, doubting a project such as *Back to the Future* would actually make it off the assembly line now, let alone hit 87mph. "The sophistication of the audience has regressed," he observed, suspecting it would no longer be possible to pitch a movie so resistant to a corporate pigeon-hole.

At least Zemeckis and his co-screenwriter Bob Gale had the sense to hold on to the creative rights, ensuring there'll be neither a sequel or remake till the pair are both dead. He regards the prospect of their collaboration being strip-mined as "outrageous": "It's like saying 'Let's remake *Citizen Kane*. Who are we going to get to play Kane?' What folly, what insanity is that? Why would anyone do that? Pre-sold title, that's the reason."

Not every film is so lucky. Over the next couple of years, audiences will be invited to turn out for retreads of *Ghostbusters, Lethal Weapon, Top Gun, Point Break, The Birds, Police Academy* and *Bill & Ted's Excellent Adventure* (didn't the new season of *Doctor Who* rip that off already?), not to mention *Star Trek 3, Star Wars VII* and Marvel's 'third phase'.

Tomorrow was yesterday.

Reviews

Poems
Iain Banks and Ken MacLeod
Little, Brown (2015)
£12.99, hardback, 162pp.
Review: Russell Jones

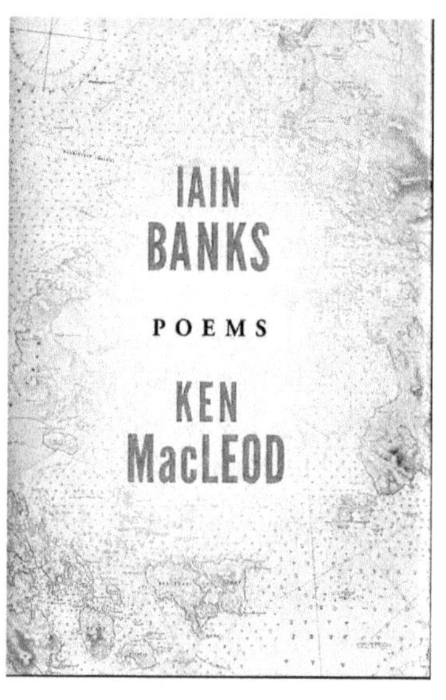

Two of Scotland's most prolific and celebrated science fiction writers, Ken MacLeod and (the late) Iain Banks join forces and book glue to produce a collection of verse: *Poems*.

This is a book of two halves, with Banks' poems appearing in the first section and MacLeod's in the second, so there are no playoffs between the two writers in terms of the book's structure. However, thematic similarities do persist, with poems about human damage and human joy. There are science fictional links too, with Banks referencing his novel *Use of Weapons* and MacLeod calling on the Morlocks of H. G. Wells, among others.

Banks' poetry maintains a definite narrative influence, switching perspectives and employing less poeticised phrasing. As such it may provide a useful doorway into the world of poetry for his fans who prefer prose. In "Extract Solenoid," for example, Banks begins part way through a story, presenting either end as "missing":

> *(missing)*
> *And peeping from the wrecks*
> *We watch the guns copulate,*
> *Flickering raps of cordite ecstasy*
> *And embarrassed cases labelled*
> *'Don't leave this lying about in...'*

Those 'missing' elements are persistent through several of Banks' poems, building an unseen narrative which allows the reader to fill in the gaps. Others are less opaque:

> *The bird is a metaphor for freedom,*
> *The bird of freedom.*
> *The book is a metaphor for life,*
> *The book of life.*

-From "Metamorphosis"

Banks' poems play with expectations, flipping meaning back on us in a linguistic game of cat and mouse (or perhaps Scouter and Destroyer). His poems are less overtly sci-fi than many of his readers might expect, with relatively few direct links to other worlds and futures. However, an alien otherness penetrates his work, making The Real seem strangely Unreal.

MacLeod's poems will more likely appeal to science fiction fans, particularly (though not exclusively) in his "A Fertile Sea" sequence, which is dedicated to Banks. Here, MacLeod's aptitude for storytelling shines through whilst also demonstrating his appreciation of linguistic depth and experiment, as well as an appreciation of the impact of the poem's form:

> *Stop the nuclear train*
> *It isn't rain it's fallout*
> *Nuclear waste fades your genes*
>   *clear was   our gen*

MacLeod's attention to the rhythm built through rhyme (train / rain) and white space ("nuclear" becomes "clear", "your genes" becomes "our gen" to show the passing of time) add an extra level of intrigue.

Whilst both poets employ longer poetic forms, MacLeod more often grasps the nettle of shorter verse to explore issues. This shows a confidence with the poetic form.

> *What does the bee feel*
> *as it clambers*
> *around the flower?*
>
> *Your hair got in my mouth*
> *your toes*
> *tickled behind my knees which now*
> *go loose as you grin at the sun*

-From "Birds and Bees and That"

Poems is something of a mixed bag in terms of consistency, but it is certainly a worthwhile exploration. It provides an alternative mouthpiece for two exceptional writers, and with that new form comes a new appreciation of their work as a whole.

If you're a fan of Banks' or MacLeod's prose, you ought to find something to appreciate in *Poems*.

Gene Mapper
Taiyo Fujii
Jim Hubbert (Translator)
Haikasoru/VIZ Media
£9.99, 240pp.
Review: Iain Maloney

In Japan Taiyo Fujii is a respected and highly-successful science fiction writer and commentator. *Gene Mapper—Core* sold ten thousand copies as a self-published e-book before being snapped up by major league publisher Hayakawa Shobo. Since then he has expanded *Gene Mapper* into a full novel, published another novel (*Orbital Cloud*) and numerous short stories. He has also won some of the biggest awards in Japanese SF, news that he was finally being translated into English was met with excitement.

Gene Mapper is a high-tech thriller set in East Asia in 2036. It is a world of augmented realities in which the characters more often than not interact through virtual spaces. Chips implanted throughout their bodies allow them to control avatars; behavioural software masks their emotions. It is also a world in which GM crops have eradicated hunger around the globe. Mamoru Hayashida is a gene mapper, a designer responsible for programming the DNA of rice crops. He freelances, something of an artist living in symbiosis with corporate Japan. He's a laid-back guy, proud of his work but content with his lot. Not the kind of man

who may hold the future direction of human society in his hand.

When mutations appear in a plantation Mamoru programmed, he is called on to investigate. He travels first to Vietnam where he enlists the services of Yagodo, a legendary hacker, before moving on to the rice fields of Cambodia. As Mamoru digs into the mutating genes it becomes clear their changes are the result of ecological terrorism. Mamoru and Yagodo are in a race against time to unmask the mastermind behind the anti-GM protestors.

The book is a thrilling page-turner packed with action and cliff-hangers but it is the ideas behind the world that most fascinates. On paper, people hiding behind technology and DNA manipulation on demand in the marketplace sound like the building blocks for a dystopian nightmare but Fujii does something fascinating with it: he builds a potential utopia.

Utopianism has a long and distinguished history in science fiction but is often shunned by writers, and with good reason: it's very hard to do well. Dystopia is easy. We are daily surrounded by people arguing that we are all off to hell in some kind of wheeled contraption or up a certain creek with a shortage of watersports equipment. A writer can take that on, run with it, show us every possible dimension ending in every possible agony. But a perfect world? We can never quite believe it: happy endings are great, but they always come at a price.

Fujii doesn't show us the realisation of his utopianism, rather he takes us to the moment when its foundations are laid. At the heart of *Gene Mapper* is the Open Source ideal: keeping information from the public is wrong. Put all information out there and let humanity decide what to do with it. It's the scientific ideal writ large across the planet and *Gene Mapper* is essentially a test case, a thought experiment into Open Source with enough explosions, chases, double-crosses and dramatic denouements to keep even the darkest pessimist entertained. This is science fiction post-Snowden and post-WikiLeaks.

In all Fujii's work there is a positivity about technology, that it provides humanity with unheralded opportunities if we are far-sighted enough to grasp them. Human history, for Fujii, is the process by which technology has made the average life better, be it medicine or social networking. His speculation is that the future will be more of the same. There's some comfort in that.

Lie of the Land
Michael F. Russell
Polygon
£12.99, hardback, 304pp
Review: Ian Hunter

I suppose horror movies have a set of 'rules' that are there to be broken, a list that would be 'don'ts' for people who don't live on the big screen or on the printed page or tablet screen. Don't go down into the cellar, don't go up into the attic, don't answer the phone, don't investigate that noise. One of the good things about Michael F. Russell's *Lie of the Land* is that his hero, investigative journalist Carl Shewan, has doggedly followed a lead and managed to get out of Glasgow to reach the sleepy little coastal fishing village of Inverlair, a place as far removed from the typical horror destinations as you can imagine; a place he really did want to get to, and that very action has saved his life. That's one of two major good things, the other is the poor mobile phone reception in Inverlair, which also saves his life. This was something that I read with a wry smile as I holiday on the East Coast of Scotland every year and know first hand how difficult it is to get a signal.

Lie of the Land gives us a slightly Orwellian alternative

future where the State watches all and surveillance is everywhere. All for our good, of course, for this is a world where the ecological disaster known as 'white rust' has happened and people have to be controlled—where they can go is restricted, and when they can do things is also restricted thanks to curfews. For Carl Shewan it can't get any worse, or so it seems, but State control is about to up a gear with the introduction of the new SCOPE super-surveillance system. Carl has heard things, snippets of bad news that are being concealed and the only way to find out for sure is to travel north out of Glasgow—which will be no mean feat in itself. To meet his informant he heads north to Inverlair because it is a 'notspot'—out of range of the mobile phone masts and transmitters.

But disaster strikes, big time (and in a way that slightly reminded me of the nano-technology gone wrong that spells the end of the world in James Lovegrove's *Shall Inherit* from the collection *Solaris Rising 2*) but fortunately Shewan is in the right place at the wrong time because when he is in Inverlair SCOPE gets activated and it has a crucial flaw, creating a brain wave like the one associated with deep sleep. Soon everyone within its range goes into a deep sleep from which they never wake up. Those in Inverlair occupy their own 'notspot' and are safe, yet if they head out of the village and start getting a signal on their phone their noses will start to

bleed, they will get one killer of a headache and then they will meet that big sleep.

Yes, it's the end of the world but not as you know it. Perhaps, more like a 'soft apocalypse' to borrow a phrase by Will McIntosh, or an 'uncosy catastrophe' to warp one by Brian Aldiss. The world ends not by alien invasion, meteor strike, or beneath the clawing hands and tearing teeth of the zombie hordes but by a technological glitch. Carl's world contracts to a place the size of the village and its beautiful surroundings Seemingly Russell chose the name Inverlair after the real Inverlair Lodge near Inverness where spies were 'parked' following the second world war. Who knows, maybe Patrick McGoohan heard about the place and went on to devise another claustrophobic village of his own.

Lie of the Land is greater than the sum of its possible parts, and those parts might be *1984*, or *Lord of the Flies*, even *Under the Dome* and certainly, with its pace and visual sense of location and landscape I was reminded of the first half of the novel *One* written by that poet of horror, Conrad Williams. Perhaps, there is no way not to mention the work of Iain Banks, in particular *A Song of Stone*. For some this will not be an easy read, though it is told in a straightforward style (reminiscent of so many reporters-turned-authors) except when Shewan encounters the natural world—that's when the prose really comes alive. The story doesn't unfold in a linear fashion, and there are times when there was a viewpoint switch that was slightly clunky, but Russell keeps us in a 'need to know' mode with a couple of cards up his sleeve even when we are following Shewan. He isn't a particularly likeable character: he's a bit of a rebel and a bit of a boozer. He's an old-fashioned journalist fighting against the system who finds himself the outsider—trapped in Inverlair as things break down, become hard and turn sour as a new order is established.

I've often wondered what happened to the protagonists in some of my favourite books. To Don Wanderley in Peter Straub's *Ghost Story* as he staggers away from a beach with a bloody hand; to Ben Mears and Mark Petrie as they light a fire in *Salem's Lot*; and to Carl Marsalis in Richard Calder's *Black Man* as he walks into the sun. To that list I can add the characters from Russell's *Lie of the Land* who are about to—to what? Well, read the book and like me, wonder what happened next. If a book can make you do that, then it's done part of its job, hasn't it?

The Promise of the Child
Tom Toner
Gollancz
£14.99, trade pb, 491 pp.
Review: Duncan Lunan

Tom Toner is a new writer, and as usual in such cases, the editor and advance readers find plenty of other writers to compare him to. Iain M. Banks's Culture novels (three times), Isaac Asimov's Foundation series, Michael Moorcock's Dancers at the End of Time, David Mitchell, Alastair Reynolds, Gene Wolfe, Jack Vance and are all invoked, while Will McIntosh and Adam Roberts tell us that it's space opera like no other!

To begin with the Asimov comparison, the novel is set in the 147th century, in 14,647 AD to be precise. 12,000 years earlier, the human race broke out to the stars. At first, recognising star designations such as Kapteyn's Star, Barnard's Star and Epsilon Indi, and recurring references to an 11 light-year battlefront, I thought they had stopped at what was defined as the first wave of interstellar colonisation, in my own Man and the Stars (Tau Ceti, at 12 l.y., is known here as The

Last Harbour); then, from a throwaway reference to a hundred settlements, it might have been the 22-light-year radius of stars evaluated in Dole's *Habitable Planets for Man*. Cryptic possible references to worlds with known exoplanets such as 'Virginis' put the boundary further out, and we're told 'Cancri' (possibly 55 Cancri, at 40 l.y.) is the outer limit. 'Virginis' might then be 61 Virginis at 27.9 l.y., but 'Aquarii', the nearest one to it, is harder to identify. Wherever it is, I can't believe that events in one constellation, as seen from here, can be seen in real-time from the other, as they are on p.197.

What stopped the expansion was the failure to find life, at even the lowest microscopic level, on any of the planets reached, even though a full quarter of them had high-oxygen atmospheres, like Earth towards the end of the dinosaur era. That and some other finds which I won't give away would have worried me a great deal, too, and perhaps it's for that reason that humans chose to go underground on many of those planets, creating 'Vaulted Worlds' with artificial suns inside. But whatever defences they had are evidently no longer working, because at the start of the novel one has been attacked and another destroyed. The attackers are alternative varieties of humans who have been produced either by adaptation or by deliberate modification on the more distant settlements which surround the

Firmament, which designates the nearer worlds ruled by advanced, long-lived humans called the Amarinthines. There are matter-transmitter links between some of these, accessible to Amarinthines only, but there are still large numbers of operational starships, taking only weeks for interstellar journeys, though they're very old and becoming decrepit. So unlike the Foundation series, where we have a galaxy filled with unmodified humans who have forgotten their origin, here we have a relatively small number and range of occupied worlds with Earth (the Old World) still playing a major rôle, though the capital is 'Gliese'—possibly Gliese 526, at 16 light-years—and the dominance of the older worlds is being challenged. Although the varieties of humans are sufficiently diverse to be regarded as aliens in some ways, they have much more in common than the many races of Iain M. Banks's Culture.

There are two main plot-lines running through the novel, both involving journeys. The first concerns a device called the Shell, which has been invented to bring war dead back to life for renewed service. I have severe doubts about the practicality of this (can you imagine what a M.A.S.H. unit would be like if it had to triage the dead as well as the living?) and it seems to invoke the concept of 'life-force,' which has been rejected in biology for at least a century (Richard Dawkins does a demolition job on it in Unweaving the Rainbow), and 'yet survives, stamped on these lifeless things' only in Torchwood and the weaker moments of Dr. Who and Star Trek. But what Tom Toner does with it is very clever, and reveals that there are much bigger and darker forces at work within the Firmament—echoing Peter F. Hamilton's The Reality Dysfunction, I thought, though no-one seems to have added that to the list of comparisons.

These forces may or may not be in contention with a new challenge to the ruler of the Firmament, whose Emperor is a recluse who has apparently lost the plot—not least because he's issued an edict authorising an investigation into the legitimacy of the Pretender, seriously undermining his own position. But among the Amarinthines seniority is decided literally, on the assumption that wisdom comes with increasing age, even though the older ones are increasingly becoming senile; and we know, if we've picked up the clues in the prologue, that the Pretender may be truly immortal and older than any of them. Echoes here of Alistair Reynolds, right enough; but as with the other comparisons, they're not close enough to be troubling.

Caught up in all this is Lycaste, who lives in a mansion among a small settlement on the coast of the Mediterranean, is in unrequited love with Pentas, the sister of one of his neighbours, and is preoccupied with building a completely accurate model of his own house. (Echoes here of *The Wasp Factory*, I thought...) We learn later that this is in the Tenth Province in a spiral outwards from the Amarinthine enclave, thousands of miles across, with inhabitants diverging further from human norms and leading increasingly lawless lives, many of them now in outright rebellion. Lycaste's less-than-happy existence is further spoiled by the arrival of Callistemon, a government census-taker from the Second Province, whom he throws from a window after the inspector forms a liaison with Pentas and sets fire to the model. Lycaste then goes on the run, wandering across large tracts of open country before blundering into violent situations in neighbouring Provinces. There are definite echoes here of Jack Vance, particularly of Cugel the Clever (which Lycaste is not), and also of

Silverberg's *Majipoor*, not the mention the Wolfe and Moorcock comparisons—nor Sheckley's *Journey of Joenes* and its 18th century inspiration, Fielding's *Tom Jones*. But all is not as it seems, or even as it seems to seem: Lycaste's saga is all part of what seems an excessively ramshackle plot to have him brought to trial in the Second Province by Callistemon's family, in order to lure out and kill the child-heir to the Firmament throne. Yet Lycaste hasn't killed Callistemon, though he checks the body for life-signs and is sure he has none, and Callistemon's family are still seeking revenge at the end of the book. Callistemon survives with only a head-wound, only to succumb to a condition which suggests that either he or Pentas are not who we've been told they are.

Of all the elements in this complex novel, I had biggest trouble with Lycaste's story. The lure to attract the boy-king is that Lycaste is outstandingly beautiful, but when he's on his travels nobody takes much notice; and if that's all it takes to bring the boy within gunshot, why not simply abduct Lycaste or bring him to the Second Province on some simpler, more reliable pretext? (As it is, Callistemon's sister nearly frustrates the entire plot by simply stabbing Lycaste in revenge.) But I was even more thrown when suddenly everbody there starts referring to him as a giant. Checking back, he is indeed a member of an advanced variety of human called the Melius, bred to serve the Amarinthines, and described in the early chapters as 'huge'. Lycaste is indeed bigger than Callistemon (a lot bigger, we suddenly learn when they come to blows), and Jotrofe, a suspected Amarinthine living in their community, is described as little. But the census-taker is in turn bigger than Pentas's sister; yet in dialogues between Lycaste and Pentas there's no hint of a difference in size which might preclude a physical relationship. To complicate things further, we're told on p.41 that 'the kingdom of the giant Melius is where they shall stay; they would never risk coming here, into the greater Firmament'. Yet Lycaste and his fellows live independent and prosperous lives, and he's not obviously different from the people he meets in neighbouring Districts before his capture, so it looks as if there's a substantial Melius presence on Earth itself, and they're not in service to anyone.

That's not the only such problem I had. We're told by Lycaste's father and others that Earth's Moon, though terraformed (the Green Moon), is off-limits. Supposedly, people there are so adapted to lunar conditions, of their own choice, that they can't come to Earth. Yet at the beginning of Part III, it seems there are Melius on the Moon, and travel between the Moon and Earth is commonplace. In a first novel, it's possible that such non-sequiturs could be a product of the rewritings which are hinted at in the Acknowledgments; but in such a complicated plot, with so much vital information given earlier in what seem at the time to be minor asides, it's possible that the confusions are only apparent and there are more clues which I've missed.

The book's title comes from Ovid, through Lycaste's father, and Lycaste applies it to his own shortcomings: "How little is the promise of the child fulfilled in the man." But we know from the very first part of the prologue, when we apparently glimpsed the Pretender in 14th century Prague, that there was another child of great promise whom he took under his wing, away back then. Will the next book clear up all these puzzles? As this is Volume One of a trilogy called *The Amarinthine Spectrum*, I suspect that Volume Two will make things still more complicated.

Swords Versus Tanks
M. Harold Page
ebook (Amazon)
Review: Elsa Bouet
This is a fast paced novel and, and as expected from the title, full of battles. The title could suggest that the wielded swords might seem archaic and would easily be obliterated by those who hold the tanks, but swords imbued with magic provide more than adequate resistance to the technologically advanced onslaught.

This novel presents three different factions at war. Taking place in the middle ages, the novel introduces us to Sir Ranulph Dacre, a knight and blood brother of the High King of the Runes Isles. His enemy is Duke John Clifford, who wants to take Ranulph's castle, lands and title. Clifford is also the nephew of the King of Westerland, whom Clifford wants to murder as he wants to accede to the throne. To further complicate the situation of this already troubled and unstable land, another force named Egality, led by a commander named Jasmine, arrives from the future. The Egality is an intergalactic force in charge of delivering freedom to all nations and end the reign of the Elitists, a group we never really meet but said to enslave the planets or nations it conquers. Each of the three sides has specific beliefs which they will use to fight those

they wish to conquer. Sir Ranulph uses the magical power of runes, Clifford bases his strength on faith and his being blessed by his priests, and the Egality uses advanced machinery and engineering. The novel therefore places what could be regarded as different levels of advancement side by side in the same historical period, annulling historical continuity to interrogate and challenge the conception of historical progress.

The narrative should not necessarily be judged by its catchy title, as there is more to it than just simple fighting. I found the first three chapters a little difficult to get into precisely because the novel throws the reader straight into descriptions of battle and because some of the descriptions in these chapters are a little repetitive—for example the insistence on Ranulph's armour and weapons being 'rune-etched'—and feel a little contrived. This focus on the battle does not provide much room for the reader to get attached to a character or to a faction. While this might potentially be a deterrent to keep on reading the rest of the novel, I think this indifference I felt for the factions or the characters provides an impartiality necessary to assess the politics at play in the novel. The story is not about the characters themselves, as they are mere political pawns. Once the novel reveals the flaws of each ideology, the imperialist attitudes, the

hypocrisy, the corruption and the hunger for power of each side, the novel becomes a compelling read. I kept on asking myself which side I thought was worse and kept on reading in quest of redeeming qualities in one of the factions.

As with other alternative history narratives, such as Philip K. Dick's *The Man in the High Castle* or Ward Moore *Bring the Jubilee*, the novel begs the reader to investigate the depicted politics, to challenge the idea of progress, to questions the ways in which we represent the past as uncivilised while mistakenly considering our present enlightened.

The novel's greatest strength lies in its engaging the reader to assess each side and raising questions. It is also a great page turner filled with secrets being revealed, plot twists and cliff-hangers, the main one occurring at the end and making me want to read the second book of *Swords Versus Tanks* very soon.

**I Am Because You Are
Pippa Goldschmidt, Tania Hershman (editors)
Freight Books
£8.99, paperback 196pp.
Review: Iain Maloney**
2015 marks one hundred years since Albert Einstein published his General Theory of Relativity although it seems like only yesterday. How time flies. To celebrate the occasion Pippa Goldschmidt and Tania Hershman have curated this collection of short stories, poetry and essays

inspired by, reacting to, or crashing against Relativity.

They are ideal editors for such a project, with impressive backgrounds in science and literature. Goldschmidt has a PhD in astronomy and her books *The Falling Star* and *The Need for Better Regulation of Outer Space* engage with science and scientists in exciting and enlightening ways. Hershman worked for years as a science journalist before turning to fiction, publishing two sparkling short story collections, *My Mother was an Upright Piano* and *The White Road*.

The book opens with a friendly introduction explaining relativity for readers who may run screaming at the word 'physics' and it's a credit to both writers' talent that it makes the theory easy to understand without ever tipping into condescension. The three

essays scattered amongst the stories also walk this fine line of clarity and insight, with Jo Dunkley's piece on cosmology in particular an exceptional example of science writing while Pedro G. Ferreira's *A Month in Berlin* displays an infectious passion for Einstein's work.

The majority of the stories in the collection were commissioned by the editors, with an open competition providing four more. Reading the biographies in the back, it's clear that some of the writers have more of a background in science than others. Perhaps as a result of this the stories fall into two categories: those that engage directly with the science and those that use Relativity as metaphor.

In the first category Neil Williamson's *Shifting* posits two potential futures for a couple of scientists in what can only be described as a Schrödinger's Baby scenario. Tasneem Zehra *Husain's Pont au Double*—one of the stand out stories in the book—takes on the problem of observation and a troubled relationship in Paris. Helen Sedgwick's *Quantum Gravity or: The Pigmy Marmoset and the Prefabricated Concrete Bungalow* strangely does exactly what it says in the title.

Arthur C Clarke's oft quoted adage that "any sufficiently advanced technology is indistinguishable from magic" could be extended to cover some scientific theories, and many of the stories take this line with Relativity. Vanessa Gebbie's *Captain*

Quantum's Universal Entertainment is as surreal and quirky a study of the theory's implications as you're likely to find. Simon Barraclough's *Ticked Off*—the only out and out genre piece in the anthology—is a terrifying story of the commodification of time. Ruby Cowling's *The Two-Body Problem* uses particle physics and unorthodox typography to examine sibling rivalry between twins.

Of course no book about Relativity would be complete without an appearance by the great man himself. Dilys Rose's excellent story *Correspondence* is a snapshot of a moment in Einstein's life, reminding us that behind one of the most important ideas our species has ever had was a very human man. The image of a son yearning for his absent father while the father's theory spreads around the globe is heartbreaking.

There is a lingering separation between science as theorised on blackboards and practiced in labs and the arts, literature in particular. Publishing and the media have long run with the narrative that there are science people and there are arts people and never the twain shall meet—a narrative that largely ignores reality, and the entire genre of science fiction— but which nevertheless has been powerful. When Ian McEwan published *Solar*, a not very good book about climate change with a Nobel-winning physicist as its main character, the mainstream literary press were up in arms at the audacity of it. Tibor Fischer, writing in the Daily Telegraph, went so far as to question whether global warming was a fit subject for fiction. In many circles it is far more acceptable to say you don't understand Relativity than to admit to never having read Shakespeare or rejecting Dickens as a third-rate waffler, a baffling state of affairs in the twenty-first century. As part of the preparation for this book the astrophysics group at Oxford University hosted a day-long workshop bringing together physicists and writers. In her recent inaugural lecture at the University of Glasgow Professor Louise Welsh spoke about the need for more fraternisation of this kind, citing collaborations between Val McDermid and forensic scientists at Dundee University. A rubicon has been crossed, it seems. Science fiction —fiction rooted in science, fiction grown from science, fiction about science—is moving into the mainstream. What we fans of science fiction have long known is becoming the norm—science and literature are ideal bed-fellows. Pippa Goldschmidt, Tania Hershman and Freight Books are to be commended for such a diverse, intoxicating, thought-provoking anthology.

MultiVerse

Russell Jones

Say "science fiction poetry" to your average Mo in the street and you'll probably receive a look of confusion, maybe even a slap in the face. The arts and sciences have frequently been pitted against one another in an academic cage fight (eye gouging allowed, crotch hits encouraged), but the fact is this: people have been writing successful science fiction poems for centuries.

In his preface to *Where Rockets Burn Through: Contemporary Science Fiction Poems* from the UK, Alasdair Gray (one of Scotland's most brilliant and bizarre writers) describes two of the world's most famous epic poems, Milton's *Paradise Lost* and Dante's *Divine Comedy*, as science fictions. He explains this in some detail, but defines his concept of science fiction for the reader:

"Fiction entertains by making parts of the life we know well wonderfully interesting, for describing wonderfully strange lives as if they were possible. Science fiction is in the second category, but differs from other fantasies by taking for granted the scientifically accepted."

Depending on your definition of science fiction (or sci-fi, SF, or whatever you might wish to call it at this hour), history is littered with poems which engage with modern, soon-to-be or potential-future technologies and sciences. From W.H. Auden

("After Reading a Child's Guide to Modern Physics") to John Donne ("Infiniteness"), Emily Dickinson ("Lightly Stepped a Yellow Star") to H.D. ("Stars Wheel in Purple"), Robert Frost ("Astrometaphysical") to Ralph Waldo Emerson ("Monadnoc"), you'll discover plenty. The difficulty is much less in finding the poems, but in their classification. Pluto faced a similar displacement during its disrobing as a planet. We're here for you, Pluto! Stay strong!

Warp forwards to nearly-modern day and your starship will collide with Edwin Morgan, the Scottish poet laureate (or Makar - until 2010, when he died). Morgan was confident in proclaiming the genre of his work, and some of his science fiction poems ("The First Men on Mercury" and In "Sobieski's Shield" for example) are frequently chosen as Reader Favourites.

Morgan believed that poetry ought to consider "man within his whole environment: not just the drop of dew; the rose, the lock of hair, but the orbiting rocket in Anselm Hollo, the laboratory in Allen Ginsberg, the lunar mountains in Hugh Mae." It is this forward-thinking attitude which pushes our art outward, not constantly looking back at heather-laden hills and dry stone walls, thinking "Oh wasn't the past wonderful?"

And so we come to the crux of the matter: why write or read science fiction poetry? My short answer is this: Art should respond to the concerns of its time. Science is an increasingly important part of modern life for most of us. We all carry tiny electronic devices which allow us to laugh with people across the globe, to instantly find out almost any piece of information, to show us amusing videos of babies and cats—we're living in a science fiction! Science fictions can also take our current preoccupations a step further—projecting contemporary issues into the future. With self-made threats such as global warming and nuclear war, this speculation seems more vital than ever.

But if you're reading this magazine, you're already onboard (welcome, lieutenant!) with the values of science fiction. A science fiction poem attempts the same things as its prose-based cousin, but in a smaller space. A quick read? You've got it! A shallow one? Probably not.

A great science fiction poem can build a world, technology or idea in a short space, whilst also using the tools of the poem (line breaks, rhyme, shape, metaphor and so on) to provide interesting twists in language and meaning. A poem is a snapshot, you fill in the reel. If fiction is a pint of lager, a poem is shot of whisky. And in our case, a shot of delicious space whisky. Mmmm, taste the quasars.

So with all that buzzing in your ion engine, I would like to introduce you to *MultiVerse*! This is Shoreline of Infinity's new platform for science fiction poetry, and will include poems from across the universe (although, primarily from Earth). Issue 2 of *Shoreline of Infinity* starts our long and scenic voyage with two behemoths of Scottish science fiction: Iain M Banks and Ken MacLeod.

Issue 3 follows with poems from (the Science Fiction Poetry Association Grandmaster) Marge Simon, and prolific US-Scotland-based writer Jane Yolen, with infinite possibilities to follow...

MultiVerse:
Iain Banks and Ken MacLeod

Iain Banks (known more commonly as Iain M. Banks to his science fiction readers) is the author of over 20 novels including *The Wasp Factory*, *The Crow Road*, *Use of Weapons*, *Consider Phlebas* and *Excession*.

I first men Iain during a book launch in Edinburgh. I wanted him to write the preface for a book of science fiction poems I was editing, called *Where Rockets Burn Through*. Nervously, I approached the signing table, his latest tome in my hand.

"Great reading, Iain, thank you for your time."

"You're welcome, dear future leader of mankind." (I'm paraphrasing here, my memory is blurry) "Who am I signing to?"

"Ebay." (That's a joke, albeit a bad and overused one) "Russell, please. I wanted to ask if you'd consider writing the preface to a book of modern sci-fi poems I'm editing."

"Oh." (He bowed his head, I seem to recall, in reverence.) "I'm no good at prefaces, and not that into poetry. Sorry."

So, imagine my surprise when I see *Poems*, published in 2015, not long after Iain's death. Between its covers? About 100 pages of poetry written by Iain Banks, and a further 60 or so from Ken Macleod.

Ken MacLeod has published over a dozen novels and pieces of short fiction, including *The Star Fraction*, *Cosmonaut Keep*, *The Cassini Division* and *Intrusion*. I first met him at the launch of my science fiction poetry pamphlet, back in 2009, where he offered some kind words of support.

Although Ken might not be well known for his poetry, his verse has appeared in print in *Poems and Polemics*, and *Where Rockets Burn Through: Contemporary Science Fiction Poems from the UK*. He's a familiar face at science fiction events, as well as being a vital, prolific and great writer in the genre.

In the Reviews section of this issue of *Shoreline of Infinity*, you'll find my opinions on Ken and Iain's book of poems, so you can find out what I thought of their dual-collection as a whole, but you now have the opportunity to read a few of their poems for yourself.

The sharp retinas among you will notice the textual references to H.G. Wells, and Iain M. (the M stands for "money" he announced at the book launch) Banks' *Use of Weapons*, but irrelevant of those contexts, the poems included here all work through building unease; there's a verge of danger and bout of war about them, which not only offers a snapshot of potential futures or other worlds, but also an emotional connection through their use of tension and The Unknown. Go forth, dive in!

Iain Banks

Zakalwe's Song

Watching from the room
As the troops go by.
– You ought to be able to tell, I think,
Whether they are going or coming back
By just leaving the gaps in the ranks.
– You are a fool, I said
And turned to leave,
Or maybe only mix a drink
For that deft throat to swallow
Like all my finest lies.
I faced into the shadows of things,
You leant against the window,
Gazing at nothing.
– When are we going to leave?
We could get stuck here,
Caught
If we try to stay too long.
(Turning)
Why don't we *leave*?
I said nothing,
Stroked a cracked glass,
Found knowledge in the silence;
The bomb lives only as it is falling.

(1973)

'Slight Mechanical Destruction'

Zakalwe enfranchised;
Those lazy curls of smoke above the city,
Black wormholes in the air of noontime's bright
Ground Zero;
Did they tell you what you wanted to be told?
Or rain-skinned on a concrete fastness,
Fortress island in the flood;
You walked amongst the smashed machines,
And looked through undrugged eyes
For engines of another war,
And an attrition of the soul and the device.
With craft and plane and ship,
And gun and drone and field you played, and
Wrote an allegory of regress
In other people's tears and blood;
The tentative poetics of your rise
From a mere and shoddy grace.
And those who found you,
Took, remade you
('Hey, my boy, it's you and us knife missiles now,
Our lunge and speed and bloody secret:
The way to a man's heart is through his chest!')
– They thought you were their playing,
Savage child; the throwback from wayback
Expedient because
Utopia spawns few warriors.
But you knew your figure cut a cipher
Through every crafted plan,

And playing their game for real
Saw through their plumbing jobs
And wayward glands
To a meaning of your own, in bones.

The catchment of those cultured lives
Was not in flesh,
And what they only knew,
You felt,
With all the marrow of your twisted cells.

(1978)

Ken MacLeod

Re-entry

unsickly wit to let the calves defend
my still calm body
but they nuzzled grass
and by their prowling kept the wolves away

into my back the flowers
shoved poppy nettle coltsfoot clover
and rosebay willow-herb
as though to re-assert
their briefly diverted mandate

the clouds had stalks, they
 not drifting in the wind
swayed

the blue was almost black
a few pernicious stars
frayed the zenith
gamma fell with the light as hail in rain

somewhere in the distance
the voices of the recovery team
nit-picking shreds of my parachute

accelerating yet, a soul passed
its final puzzled words:
'But I thought Engels –'

the only heaven is annihilation

around me the module burned
its scattered fragments indecipherable

(1975)

The Morlock's Arms

The wasps are big this year, the meteors
green in the summer night. Our land
ironclads are far away, our flying-machines
visit atrocity on innocence. We do not care.
This is the World State. We're a planet now.

Our empire was the sun,
famine or fusillade its worst extreme,
its best a world that turned
on a war we fought, in the air.

And we're still here, in the light,
we Morlocks, we whose corpses
rotted conveniently in the cosy catastrophe,
we feckless, toothless proles, feral cattle
for whom entropy was never cool.

No Empire now, nor New Jerusalem,
no Modern Utopia. Only the streets
of Earth and England

and a sense of something about to happen.
Because we never went away
we will think of something
in our own time, gentlemen. Please.

(2000)

IN THE EMPTY PLACES

• Short Stories and Art •

An exciting and diverse collection by award-winning writers and artists from around the world, some translated into English for the first time. Available as an ebook (€5) or paperback (€15).

Featuring new work from Toni Davidson, Rodge Glass, Rodrigo Hasbún, Tendai Huchu, Kirsty Logan, Anneliese Mackintosh, Iain Maloney, Monica Metsers, Suhayl Saadi, Simon Sylvester, and Chiew-Siah Tei plus many more.

The Bantuan Coffee Foundation provides safe houses and education scholarships for the victims of child prostitution in Indonesia.
www.bantuancoffee.org

•

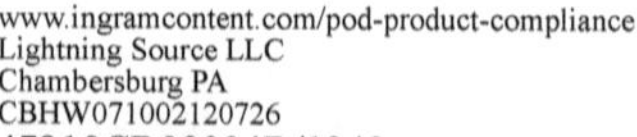
www.ingramcontent.com/pod-product-compliance
Lightning Source LLC
Chambersburg PA
CBHW071002120726
47910CB00004B/1342